WHERE
THERE'S
SMOKE

THE MONTANA FIRE SERIES:

Where There's Smoke
Playing With Fire
Burnin' For You
Oh, The Weather Outside is Frightful (novella)

MONTANA FIRE
SUMMER OF FIRE TRILOGY

1

WHERE THERE'S SMOKE

SUSAN MAY WARREN

sdg

SDG PUBLISHING

A division of Susan May Warren Fiction

Minneapolis, MN

PRAISE FOR WHERE THERE'S SMOKE BY AMAZON.COM READERS

The Montana Fire series is off to a thrilling start that will have you on the edge of your seat!

The new Montana Fire summer series by Susan May Warren is off to a blazing hot start. Book one, Where There's Smoke, is the story of Blazin' Kate Burns, a smokejumper following in her fathers' footsteps, determined to prove she can make it in this male-dominated field and Jed Ransom, fire boss and her fathers' protégé who will stop at nothing to keep her safe, including resisting his love for her.

The unique and original storyline begins with characters at odds with each other who are forced to work closely together while working out their personal differences and end up ultimately having to work out their bigger issues with God. In classic Warren style, what starts as an entertaining and thrilling read becomes not only an opportunity to contemplate Kate and Jed's choices, but the catalyst for their transformation as well. I love how Warren always brings the reader back to spiritual observations and insights.

For those of us who are Susan May Warren fans, it was fun to see how she tied the much loved Christiansen series into this new one. Darek Christiansen was, for a time, on the same Jude County hotshot team with Jed Ransom as was Luke Alexander from the novella, *You Don't Have to Be a Star.*

Playing With Fire, book two, features smoke jumper Conner Young, who was also in Warren's Team Hope series and Liza Beaumont from the Christiansen and Deep Haven series.

Burnin' for You, book three, features smoke jumper Reuben Marshall and pilot Gilly Priest.

Terrific summer reading until Warrens' Mercy Falls, Montana search and rescue team adventure series begins with Wild Montana Skies. Can hardly wait! ~ *Tracey* book corner fan, Amazon.com reader

A sizzling start to the series!

This series is full of action and drama, like a hang-on-to-your-seat (or parachute, if you will), thrill ride from start to end. In the middle of the chaos, moments of slightly sizzling romance (while always remaining classy), deep emotion, and strong messages of faith unfold.

"Complex" doesn't begin to describe the tangle of history between Jed and Kate. It was established off page and opens this story with action and tension, with ties to fire and a mutual history, both deeply respectful of Jock Burns (Kate's dad).

Susan works references to fire and parachuting all over the place, and it works so well! Like this quote: "He wasn't sure how he'd gone from standing at the edge of her world to an all-out dive into what he'd been quietly longing for his entire life, but he wasn't going to look up, see a possible tear in his canopy." (from chapter 7)

Main theme/lesson: Learning to cling to faith, that God is always to sustain you. ~*Camera Courton*, Amazon.com reader

Susan May Warren Never Disappoints!

Every time I see a new book by Susan May Warren, I absolutely MUST have it! I treasure her novels. She writes with an amazing depth and a true, powerful spiritual message. It's like sitting down and hearing a wonderful message at church!

Blazin' Katie Burns is a legendary smokejumper, known for her courage and willingness to risk everything to get the job done. But she has a secret she won't admit to anyone....

Supervisor Jed Ransom commands the Jude County Smoke Jumpers with a reputation as a calm, level-headed leader. Kate is the only one who has ever gotten under his skin. But Jed has some issues, too.

A raging wildfire in the mountains of Montana bring Kate and Jed together to train a new team of jumpers. They must now face the past they have been running from and the secrets that keep them apart. An arsonist goes after their team and they must face their deepest fears.

This is the first book of the Montana Fire series and I am so happy there are three books!

Susan May Warren has such a heart for God and it shows in the pages of her novels. She creates characters that nearly jump off the pages at the reader and dig deep into their heart. She takes you into the scenes, into the forest that is ablaze till you nearly feel that *you're* the one running from the wild fire that's threatening to take your life.

I loved every single minute of this book, couldn't wait to finish it and now I can't wait for the next! ~*Susan Snodgrass,* Amazon.com reader

Montana Fire
Summer of Fire Trilogy
Book One: *Where's There's Smoke*
ISBN-13: 978-1-943935-13-0
Published by SDG Publishing
15100 Mckenzie Blvd. Minnetonka, MN 55345
Copyright © 2016 by Susan May Warren

For more information about Susan May Warren, please access the author's website at the following address: www.susanmaywarren.com.

Published in the United States of America.

For Your glory, Lord

S HE'D COME THREE THOUSAND miles to burn to death.

"Kate, if you don't deploy right now, you're going to die!"

Kate Burns could hear Jed, his voice muffling around in the back of her brain, but the roar of the fire simply had her by the throat. Three-hundred-foot flame lengths chewing up the pristine Alaskan wilderness, torching Fraser firs, white pines, black spruce. The blaze candled along the tops of the birch trees, the fire storm churning up its own wind.

It felt like that hand of God, reaching out to grab her in a paralyzing chokehold. It kept her brain from firing, from reacting to Jed's words.

From reaching for her shake-and-bake fire shelter, folded and tucked in the pocket of her jump pants.

Because, what would it matter? They were in the green, a highly combustible area, and they'd bake to death under the thin tinfoil even if the fire didn't scurry underneath and scorch them.

And that vivid picture had her knees buckling.

Her father would be so angry.

"Kate!"

Hands on her shoulders shook her, jerked her around. "Get your shelter on!"

Kate got a glimpse of Jed a second before he threw her to the ground. Face blackened, his eyes fierce, red bandanna pulled up over his nose. And balancing hard on a makeshift crutch she'd fashioned for him only hours before.

He looked like she felt—wrung out, broken, and on the edge of unraveling.

Except, he wasn't standing still, waiting for the wall of flame to hit him. In fact, he had his shelter out, already unfurled, and now shook it over her. She fell to the ground, an old, dry riverbed, filled with gravel and rock, moss and brush. But, where he pushed her down, mostly sand and dirt.

"Pin it down! Remember your training."

Training. Oh—the three years as a hotshot—a wildland firefighter—and her last six weeks with the Midnight Sun Smokejumpers where, two weeks ago, she'd passed her final exam.

Don't die. Her training boss said it as he'd handed her the Midnight Sun patch. Laughter. She'd grinned.

Jed landed in the dirt next to her, having apparently yanked her shelter from her pocket. He wrestled with it in the superheated winds, his teeth gritted as he yanked it down to the earth. Pinning it there with hands, elbows, knees, feet.

Except, in a flash that struck her in the heart, she knew the truth.

She might not die, but Jed Ransom didn't have a prayer of holding down all four corners, not to mention the edges, of his shelter. Not with his injured leg.

Not with those bare hands.

Kate threw off her shelter and, in a second, it caught the wind and flew—no turning back now.

"What are you doing!"

She didn't answer him as she rolled herself under his

tinfoil, grabbing a corner, drawing it over her. She clamped down her side with her hand, elbow, and leg.

He caught on fast. Or maybe not as much as she'd hoped, because even as she nailed down the side with her limbs, he covered her upper body with his, protecting her.

She felt the length of his body against her, his powerful arms, honed from chopping through the dense forest, digging fire line with his fire ax, aka Pulaski. For a second, her heart just stopped with the sense of it. She'd spent the last decade wishing she might end up right here.

In Jed Ransom's arms.

Hopefully right before he kissed her.

Except, maybe she'd omit the part where they would bake.

Jed secured the top of the shelter with his hands, the other side with his elbow, knee, his good leg.

Then, her helmet crushed next to his, he said in his low baritone, "Dig us a hole to breathe into."

Outside, the fire cycloned around them, exploding through the trees into a storm of flame, the sound of it a locomotive ready to drive over them.

Kate started to shake as she clawed at the ground, scrubbing away pebbles and stone, finding the cool riverbed. She widened the hole for him, and his whiskers brushed her face as he fought to find cooler air.

"Deeper. We need to protect our faces." He balanced his helmet on the rim of the hole, his breath on her skin as he turned to her. "We're going to live, Kate, I promise."

She longed to believe him.

The 'shake and bake' flapped, the fury of the fire starting to bake them. Sweat dripped down her face, saturated her body under her jumpsuit and turnout jacket.

And then Jed's breathing caught. Tiny sounds, a deep groan as the heat began to sear his skin. But she couldn't lift her head, because suddenly the fire washed over them, a wave of heat and flame and fury that made her press her face to the earth.

She didn't know who screamed first.

CHAPTER 1

Seven years later...

Not until she reached four thousand feet did Kate Burns realize this jump had "epic comeback" written all over it. Except, her father's memorial service probably wasn't the right time to show the world that fear couldn't keep her grounded. And, with Reuben and Conner nearly out the door of the Twin Otter, herself next in line, probably it was too late to pull the plug on their commemorative jump.

But she could hardly turn down Miles Defoe, her father's incident commander. Say *no* to the entire population of Ember Montana on hand to remember the firefighters who died on a mountain last summer.

Of course she would jump. But she'd keep it safe and easy and channel the fear fisting her chest, pumping fire into her veins. Not newsworthy. Not spectacular. Not epic.

Something her father might—if he were watching from heaven—be proud of.

Over the intercom, Gilly's voice cut through the thunder of air whipping into the open door and over the drone of the plane. "I've reached four thousand!"

Kate glanced into the cockpit where Gillian Priest, her dark auburn hair looping through the hole in her gimme cap, manned the controls. Gilly glanced over her shoulder, the headphones dwarfing her, and met Kate's eyes. Grinned. A comrade-in-arms in this male-dominated world of smoke-jumping.

A paltry handful of women managed to climb the ranks and earn a spot on one of the fourteen teams around the nation. Despite the tremor in her gut or the acrid taste of bile lining her throat, Kate planned on holding onto hers with the tenacity of any of the wildland fires she'd jumped over the past seven years.

She swallowed the bile away. At least today's jump didn't require her to fly over smoky columns of superheated air. Or to drop into a blackened meadow or dirt-edged moraine just outside the roar of the dragon.

Today she didn't have to fear dying under a piece of high-tech tinfoil.

Instead, adorned with a purple memorial ribbon attached to her pack, she'd drop out of the sky in memory of seven comrades who'd perished doing what they loved.

Wearing their standard Kevlar jumpsuits and gear packs, fellow jumpers Conner Young and Reuben Marshall edged up to the door. They snapped on their helmets and peered out into the expanse.

The two men, along with Pete Brooks preparing to jump behind her, were the only survivors of her father's crew. Guys she planned on getting to know if she hoped to seal the canyon Jock Burn's death left in her heart.

She should have been jumping with him on his crew instead of returning home to honor his memory.

"Coming around for the jump," Gilly said into the coms.

Breathe. Again, Kate ran her four-point check—drogue release handle in clear view, Stevens connection attached to the reserve, reserve emergency handle in clear and plain view, and the cutaway clutch, also readily accessible.

Just stay calm. Jumping was the easy part, right? The part she actually *liked.* She reached for her helmet, glancing at her jump partner. Pete, his blond hair pulled back in a jaunty knot, blue eyes and a bronze ring of whiskers, grinned at her with a lazy smile that probably knocked the girls silly down at the Hotline Saloon.

She grinned back, offered a thumbs-up, keeping it friendly, not flirty. After all, she knew better than to fall for firefighters. Especially the make and type of charmer Brooks, with his wide football shoulders, lean torso, powerful jumper-honed legs. Jumpers like him wore danger in their eyes, and the spark that drew them to engage in battle against the demons of nature turned them into men who played hard, wooed with abandon, and lived as if every night might be their last. Until the siren sounded and fifteen minutes later, girded for combat, they disappeared into a boiling sky.

Besides, the last—and only—jumper she'd fallen for had taken her heart and hadn't the decency to return it.

She pulled on her goggles then strapped on her helmet, her vision gridded by the mask over the front. The cool air whistled into her ears.

"Let's go!" This from Conner Young a second before he pushed hard out the door, rolling right, away from the plane. Seconds later, Reuben followed.

She scooted up to take her place at the door, bracing her hands on either side of the opening, glancing out to see Reuben as he dove, spread eagle, flying toward the earth. Reuben seemed more bear than man, quiet, dark, and still harboring open wounds at seeing his crew devastated.

Survivor's guilt.

It had nothing on Estranged Daughter guilt.

Four thousand feet below, Kate spotted the little town of Ember, population thirteen hundred. A snug collection of ranch houses, restaurants, a few gift shops, a school, police station, courthouse, motel, and huge RV park made up their firefighting community nestled at the edge of the Kootenai National Forest in northwestern Montana. And right in the center of town, the towering spire of the Ember Community Church, where she'd drawn her name in the freshly poured cement of the front steps, played youth group games in the basement, and first learned what it felt like to be part of a town whose very name meant fire.

Someday, maybe, she'd go back to that little white church, find the faith her father had tried to embed in her.

To the north of town, she located their landing spot, the meadow just south of the practice towers of Ember Fire Base, home of the Jude County Wildland Firefighters.

Beyond that, in a curve of a ledge rock set at the far edge of the fire base, stood a copper likeness of a lone firefighter leaning on his Pulaski, hard hat pushed back, bedraggled, solemn, his gaze directed to the jagged, black backbone of Glacier National Park.

The Jock Burns Memorial.

She couldn't see them, but she knew the faces of the people who assembled on folding chairs around the memorial. Fresh recruits and veterans dressed in the green fire-retardant pants, the bright yellow shirts, hard hats perched on their knees, and hundreds of locals—fathers and mothers, wives and girlfriends—who understood too acutely the cost of fighting wildland fires in the West.

At the podium would be Incident Commander Miles Dafoe, eulogizing the lost, embellishing the legends. Offering condolences, stories, and, most of all, avoiding the woefully feeble attempts to answer the lingering, brutal questions of what happened that horrific night in Eureka Canyon.

How could seven able-bodied men not see the fire charging behind them, not run, not even deploy their fire shelters?

Worse, how could legendary strike team commander, smokejumping squad leader, and Ember Base Incident Commander Jock Burns, a man who could read fire as if it burned inside him, have led them to their deaths?

The tragedy still seemed incomprehensible. Even now, nearly ten months later, the town still reeled, a murmur of disbelief behind every conversation.

And underlying it all, rumblings about the wisdom of starting up another smokejumping team.

Kate refused to let her father's legacy die just because he had. Not when she could come home and keep the dream alive.

No matter how much the fear might reach up and try to strangle her.

This one's for you, Dad. She gulped a long breath, forced her stomach back down her throat. An over-the-shoulder look at Pete. He gave her a go-ahead nod, so she pulled hard out the door and flung herself into the deep.

The breath of heaven engulfed her, and as usual she longed to scream, part joy, part bone-ripping terror.

And then, the fear dropped away and she was just...flying.

Soaring above the earth, her face to the wind, her arms flung out in a wild embrace.

For seven long seconds she outran her regrets, her tomorrows full and rich with fresh starts.

Two seconds out of the plane, she started the count—*Jump Thousand.*

Wind, roaring in her ears. She rolled right, saw Pete frame the door.

Look Thousand—and look she did, despite the tilted horizon, the world whirling beneath her. A blur of splendor woven from the great troughs of the rich green Douglas fir forest trenched out by ancient glaciers. She spotted the cobalt-blue lakes tucked into hidden highland crannies and ran her gaze along the bony spine of the Great Rocky Mountains of Glacier National Park rutting up to reef the dome of the sky.

Reach Thousand. She flung her right hand back, used muscle memory to latch onto the rip cord. The other hand she stretched out, a last grasp of firmament.

Wait Thousand. One more second to soar over the grasslands of the moraine valley, pinioned by towering ponderosa pine and dissected by highways and stale brown pastures that evidenced the bone-dry spring.

Then a quick glance again to locate Pete, soaring twenty feet away. He flashed her a thumbs-up.

Pull Thousand. A final, unfettered cool gulp of stratosphere. Then she yanked, hard.

Her fall arrested with a jerk, her heart caught as the chute sailed her into the yonder. She flung her head back, watching the canopy billow out, a rectangular red cloud.

The surreal, abrupt silence rang in her ears. She checked the rear corners of the chute then reached for her steering toggles to come around into the wind.

Her gaze fell again on the red-striped plane as it disappeared into the wink of the sun.

Below, she spotted Conner and Reuben's canopies already engorged, sailing along the wind currents toward the drop zone.

Maybe she'd give the crowd a little show, come in fast,

roll hard, spring back to her feet, lithe and graceful, a move her father had perfected.

A trickle of color caught her peripheral vision.

No.

Pete Brooks was falling from the sky.

His pilot chute trailed, an impotent bubble flapping in the wind, unable to disgorge the main chute from its lodging.

"Pull your reserve!"

Her words died long before they reached him. But Pete had logged more than fifty jumps over the past two years under Jock Burn's judicious eye and, without needing her words in his ear, he deployed his reserve.

The canopy whistled up past the balloon, filled, and with a snap, Pete fluttered up into the blue, safe.

Never leave your partner.

Jed Ransom's voice in her head, the man breaking the ban to never again haunt her. His deep baritone had crawled into her head a week ago and lodged there, like he belonged.

And before she could protest, along came the memories.

Jed, holding the toggles in his strong hands, his dark hair curly out of the back of his helmet, circling her like a hawk to check her positions. Jed, those smoky blue eyes on her, following her all the way to the drop zone, shouting instructions to assist her landing. Jed, his whisper against her neck as he found her at Grizzly's.

I didn't leave you, Jed. You left me.

The familiar argument flickered, then died just as she heard the shout.

Pete wrestled with his fresh canopy, pulling at the tangled lines of *two* canopies, flapping, twisting, flattening.

It took just a second to piece it together—his pilot chute

had finally torn free from his main canopy, but the main then tangled into his reserve. A dual chute failure, and in a moment Pete would auger straight down into the meadow, die right in front of a grieving town.

His plummet was arrested only by the drag of his partially filled reserve.

No time to actually think, for panic to grab a foothold. Just— "I'm coming to you!" She angled toward him then cut her chute away.

Free falling, once again.

She hit Pete hard, scrabbled to hold on as they plummeted together.

"Grab onto me!"

He barely had his hands tucked into her pack, his legs wrapped around her, when she reached around him and cut away his chutes.

With a jerk, they fell together, the wind turning to fire in her ears.

"Hold on!" She yanked her reserve.

The lines trickled out and she braced herself.

The lift nearly yanked her from Pete's grasp. But his leg lock had the makings of a UFC welterweight champ, and the pack held, burning her arms, her shoulders, sucking out her breath. The canopy deployed, billowed full, a cloud of white against the blue expanse.

Silence, save for the thunder of her heart, his hard breathing whiffling in her ear.

"It's okay, Pete. I got you."

He raised his head and met her eyes. "I have to admit, this is my new version of best first date ever!"

She rolled her eyes. "Hold on! I'm going to try and drive

us into the wind!"

He adjusted against her, and she wished she could help him hold on, but she had her hands full hoping to slow them down, capture any cushion she could manage for their impact. A quarter mile or less below, she noticed memorial attendees rising, a few running toward the field.

They'd fallen past Reuben and Conner, now aloft above them.

"I have to admit, your dad was right about you," Pete said in her ear.

Her father had talked about her? She kept her voice cool. "How's that?"

"Let's just say he said you had more guts than any of the men he jumped with."

She didn't let her expression betray the truth.

"Listen," she said. "You're too heavy for us to land together. I can't hold you up. I'll try and angle us in—as soon as your feet touch, push away and roll. We might both live through this if we don't crash together."

"Always the Dear John. Me and my broken heart."

And there he was, charmer Pete, back in the game.

Except, his voice pitched suddenly low. "Thanks, Kate—you didn't have—"

"Of course I did. I'm your jump partner."

"But—"

Their feet dragged against the high grass and she gave him a hard push.

He fell away, and out of the corner of her eye she saw him tuck and roll. Then she was landing, rolling, bouncing back to life in a graceful, Jock Burns-style landing.

Pete too bounded to his feet like he might be an acrobat,

their stunt planned.

An uncomfortable twitter, then clapping began to undulate across the crowd.

Kate tore off her helmet, grabbing up her parachute in one swift motion as Conner and Reuben landed behind her.

She tried not to let her knees turn to liquid, her pulse thundering.

They'd lived. Sometimes, she still couldn't believe how her luck held.

"Are you kidding me?" Conner's voice. She jerked around, found him, running over to her, his helmet under his arm, his blond hair matted. He threw his arms around her, nearly knocking her off her feet. "Are you kidding me?"

She held on, just for a second, righting herself as the smattering of applause turned to cheering around her.

Breathe.

"That was crazy brave!" This from Reuben, his dark brown hair tucked into a red bandanna. He wore a rare smile. Bigger than Conner, wider shoulders, solid girth, the sawyer for the team rode bulls in his off time, bore the cowboy swagger of the men who grew up on western Montana ranches. "I swear, when I saw Pete's chutes tangle, I was sick. And then, like the Green Hornet, there you were, racing across the sky. Sheesh, if I didn't know better, I would have thought it was old Jock to the rescue." He shook his head. "Like father, like daughter, I guess."

The smallest edge of a smile tugged at her mouth, the rattle of her pulse slowing.

Then Pete bounded up. "That," he said, "is how it's done!" He high-fived Conner and Reuben and then leaned down and grabbed her face in his hands. Kate recognized his intent a second before he popped her a kiss—quick and fast.

She had no response as he backed up, his eyes shining. "No wonder they call you Blazin' Kate Burns. Honey, you can save my sorry hide any day, any time."

Then he hiked his arm around her neck. "Welcome back to Ember."

The assembly roared, then, cheered. Jock Burns's daughter was home where she belonged. The legacy, resurrected.

She lifted her hand to wave.

It was then she saw him, moving through the crowd at high speed, pushing back spectators, his face a knot of emotions, most of which she couldn't name. Panic? Worry? Surprise?

No, fury.

Because as he broke free, the emotion tightened, focused into a posture she knew too well—the darkness in his smoky blue eyes, the set of his jaw, smattered now with the finest hint of dark stubble, his fists clenched and looking every inch like a man on fire, ready to scorch the earth.

Jed Ransom.

Seven years hadn't dented his stun power. Dark, shorter hair than she remembered, the slightest disobedient curl at the temples. Wide shoulders, tapering down to a lean torso, arms that filled out his yellow Nomex shirt, lean legs that had once chased her down, saved her life.

Yes, Jed Ransom knew how to destroy a woman, make her hand over her heart with one soul-piercing look.

She'd thought the past seven years had healed her, remade her, and that she wasn't the same young jumper who ignited at the sight of him striding across the tarmac.

Kate could still remember the sound of his voice in her ear.

Apparently she was wrong.

More, she could swear she could still read his mind, because his parting epitaph from seven years ago rose inside her, soft, dark, and deadly. *Stay away from me, Kate.*

He planted himself in front of her, breathing hard. Sweat trickled down from his temple, his face just a little white. He didn't bother to whisk the sweat away or even glance at Pete, and when he swallowed, hard, she recognized his telltale attempt to rein it all in.

Look who was a little panicked. Interesting.

Kate couldn't help it. "Hey, Jed."

His blue eyes narrowed. Then, as quiet as smoke, he leaned forward and whispered in her ear, the heat of his breath on her skin. "You just don't know when to quit, do you?"

Actually...

He kept his voice low, however, for her ears only. "Well, I do. Kate Burns...pack your bags. You're fired."

Jed just needed a breath. A moment to get somewhere to press his hand to his chest, move his heart back into place, restart it.

To erase from his brain the sight of the woman he loved cutting away her parachute and free-falling to save a man twice her size.

Dumb, stupid, amazing luck—Kate lived on it. But one day her faith in luck, or God, or whatever propelled her to live life on the cusp of death, would run out. And he couldn't bear to watch.

"You can't fire me!" Her voice chased him down, and he didn't have to turn around to see her expression. Her gray-green eyes on fire, her dark red hair pulled back in a lush ponytail, the jumpsuit effectively hiding her curves, along with the muscle cultivated from years of jumping out of airplanes, fighting fires. Tough, brave and currently angry enough to take him apart, right here, in front of the entire town of Ember.

Don't react. Not with the congregation—widows, children, his fellow hotshots and jumpers—still within earshot, on hand to remember the seven smokejumpers who'd lost their lives precisely because of this kind of irresponsible, rash bravado.

The kind of bravado that Kate embodied. Clearly, it ran in the family, from Jock right down into the veins of his red-headed, hotshot daughter. No one but Jed had any idea the trouble she could cause.

The crowd parted for him as if he might be combustible.

"You can't fire me for saving Pete's life! That's crazy!"

Clearly ignoring his blatant hint that he didn't want to discuss it, she was catching up fast, even while dragging her parachute and gear. Despite the fact that she couldn't be more than one-hundred-twenty pounds soaking wet, she possessed grit that made packing out eighty-five pounds for miles through charred and desolate forest seem like a stroll through the park.

How he would love to round on her and tell her exactly what kind of *crazy* she embodied. But that would hardly win him any friends, not after her spectacular save.

What Ember didn't know was that kind of bravado could be infectious—especially for recruits—and suddenly he'd have a mess of impulsive alpha-jumpers trying to prove themselves up to Kate's standards.

And die trying.

Hadn't they all suffered enough?

"Jed!" He felt a hard tug on his arm. "Don't walk away

from me!"

Fine. He stopped short so that she nearly slammed into him. But she righted herself, still quick on her feet, and stared up at him. *Bring it*, her expression said.

Oh no. Kate still possessed the power to undo him, to sweep away coherent thought, and for a second, staring down at her, a buried memory flashed. The smell of her—pine, smoke, the rush of the sky, her own scent seeping into him. The feel of her body shaking, her head buried next to his as they fought for their lives under a fire shelter. For one terrifying day, somewhere back in time on an Alaskan mountainside, they'd belonged together.

Breathe. "Not here," he managed, hating the tremble in his voice.

"You're not the boss—oh, I forgot. Jed Ransom, fire god, ruler of hotshots and jumpers alike, supreme commander of smoke, fire, and ash." She made a mock bow and his jaw tightened. "The world bows to your divine will."

"Nice, Kate," he growled, real low. "Thanks for that." He shook his head. "But for your information, I *am* the new jump boss, in charge of training the recruits, and no, I'm not firing you for saving Pete—of course not. But let's not pretend that you both living through that *wasn't* ridiculous luck. The last thing our recruits need is the idea that they're invincible. Accidents happen when jumping, and especially now this crew has to be twice as careful. And you take too many risks."

He looked around at their audience, now tactfully dispersing, but he couldn't miss the sight of Gemma Turnquist holding her six-month-old son, the one who'd never meet his father. Or Alyssa North, still wearing her engagement ring. He'd finally thrown away the invitation to her October wedding. Or Patrick Browning, their A/P aircraft mechanic, still hollow after the loss of his son, Tom.

The next crew of smokejumpers and hotshots had to be smarter, stronger, faster, and better prepared than any other team in the history of the Jude County Wildland Firefighters.

He whirled away from her and lengthened his strides across the compound toward Overhead, the air-conditioned headquarters. He just needed to get inside, back to his world of topography maps, satellite images, computer-generated fire scenarios, and shift boards.

A world he could chart, plan, organize, and control.

A world that didn't include Kate Burns unraveling him in front of the entire town.

As usual, Kate wouldn't take no for an answer. She scrambled up next to him, walking double time. "Wait one doggone minute. Are you saying I'm a *bad influence?*"

"That's *exactly* what I'm saying."

"Some might say that I'm exactly the influence you need. Someone who can think under pressure, who isn't afraid to—"

"Risk her life over and over? Do something completely cracked?" *Oh, stop talking.* He ground his jaw and willed himself to keep his mouth shut.

"If that's what it takes."

I'm doing my best here, Jock. "Not on my watch. Somebody has to keep you from fulfilling your death wish. Like father, like daughter."

Her mouth opened, and he winced. He hadn't quite meant it that way, but he might still be reeling just a little from her appearance in the sky. Or back in his life.

He could have used an earlier heads-up from Miles, however. More than a *by-the-way, I hired Jock's daughter to train the recruits,* a comment made just before the incident commander spoke at the dedication ceremony.

Over my dead body. Jed might have even spoken those

words aloud.

Now Kate glared at him. "I'm not going to slap you, out of respect for Dad, who, for some inane reason, considered you a son." She shook her head, her expression carrying so much sting in it she might as well have slapped him. And he deserved that, probably, for reasons beyond his rude comment.

He struggled to school his voice. "You know I loved your dad. But Jock lived way too long on borrowed time."

"One mistake shouldn't define your entire legacy—you should know that better than anyone."

He sucked in a breath, and she raised an eyebrow, clearly referring to their last explosive argument, still vivid after seven years.

"This is not about Jock's death. This is about healing and the future of the Jude County smokejumpers."

"But you haven't jumped for—"

"I remember the last time I jumped, Kate."

Her face reddened. Yes, they both knew—and clearly had done a lousy job of forgetting.

"Besides, I thought you were in Boise, working in the Fire Command center. Fire Behavior Analyst, right?"

Just a flash of surprise crossed her face.

Yes, he'd kept track of her, too. And shoot, maybe he shouldn't have revealed that tidbit of information. "I don't need you here, trying to prove something," he continued before she could grab onto his words. "Like maybe your dad was wrong about you?"

That flushed all the nice out of her, and her voice turned razor-edged. "I'm here for the same reason you are. To make sure my father's legacy doesn't die with those men on the mountain." Kate's glare burned into him, the dare back in her eyes. "Besides, you need me. With the drought and the lack of snow cover this winter, this just might be the hottest summer Montana's seen in fifty years. You'll need every man—and woman—you can get to keep the state from going up in flames."

She had him there, and she probably knew it. With Montana tinder-dry, Overhead bristled at every thunderhead, jumping every time lightning struck in nearby Glacier National Park, the Bob Reserve, the Swan Range, or their very own Kootenai National Forest right outside their back door. They'd called in the contingency of veteran hotshots and a handful of smokejumpers a month earlier than usual, had the fleet of Twin Otters and Air tankers tuned up and airworthy.

"Fine. Yes, I do need you—but I don't want you anywhere near my recruits. And as for joining the team—well, just do your job and stay out of my way."

She rolled her eyes. "And here we go again." She glanced at his hands, the deformed flesh. "You still blame me."

He drew in a breath, held it. "I never blamed you," he said quietly.

Her mouth tightened, and even he could hear the echo of their fight.

"This—we are a mistake— Stay away from me, Kate."

Then, as if she could read his mind, she raised her helmet. "You're not getting rid of me that easily, Jed Ransom. Not this time. I promise, by the end of the summer, you'll be *begging* me to stay."

Then she turned and strode away, toward the memorial and the throng of fans.

He just stood there fearing she might be right.

CHAPTER 2

KATE WANTED TO THROW a small party for the tax-payers of Jude County who had invested in the private shower area for the female hotshots. Few of them as there were, and despite working just as hard, they still couldn't be one of the guys.

She stood in the stall, still shaking, her stomach freshly emptied. Now, with her hands braced against the wall, the water hot on her skin, she closed her eyes and tried not to relive every terrifying second of her free fall to Pete.

Oh, what had she been thinking?

She sank down under the water before her knees buckled and leaned her head back, letting the spray hit her face, her shoulders, drowning out the sudden hiccups of breath.

You take too many risks.

How many times had she heard that echo thrumming through her? And to see Jed's face—she'd scared them both, clearly. He was nearly white, and when he'd rounded on her outside Overhead, his eyes wide, trembling, his voice so lethal it could slice through her like a blade—it brought her right back to that moment.

Standing paralyzed as a wall of flame roared toward her.

Now, the rush of it all converged, blew apart, and she

pressed her hands over her mouth before any sobs leaked out.

After her altercation with Jed, she'd barely made it to the bathroom, leaving her jump gear in the locker room. After throwing up, she raced for the shower, hoping a towel might magically appear by the time she emerged. Which might be never if she didn't get herself under control. She let herself sob into her hands because—well, she couldn't fall apart in front of her crew, right?

Somebody has to keep you from fulfilling your death wish. Like father, like daughter.

She really wanted to hurt Jed for that comment. Except maybe it hurt him as much to say it—after all, he had loved Jock like a father, right? He'd been just as decimated by Jock's anger back when they'd nearly died in Alaska.

I never blamed you.

Hardly—he completely, utterly blamed her for everything, from his broken ankle to their near death in the shelter, to the long cold night in the woods, to her father nearly taking him apart, piece by piece.

If he hadn't blamed her, things might have turned out much differently.

She might have been able to patch things up, come home.

Instead, it had been Jed who managed to repair the rift and return to Ember, working across the hall from Jock for the last seven years.

Kate straightened up, feeling hollow, and turned off the shower. Peeked out past the curtain, and miracles! A towel fairy had hung a clean white towel just outside the shower. She grabbed it, towel-dried her hair, and wrapped the towel around her.

Gilly sat on the bench outside the shower stall, unlacing her boots. "I missed the show, Supergirl," she said. "Although apparently it wasn't as fun as the guys made it sound." She offered a sympathetic smile.

"It's just the adrenaline rush," Kate said, digging into her bag for a comb and finding none.

"I'm not judging you. Frankly, I'd probably be in the fetal position right now, so you get points for standing. But if you feel like buying out all the Ben and Jerry's at the local convenience store, I'm your wingman." She got up, tugged off her hat, and unzipped her jumpsuit. "By the way, I think Pete wants a date. He's singing your praises out there, saying you were just looking for an excuse to get your hands on him."

Kate rolled her eyes, and Gilly laughed.

"Fear not, I told him that you know better than to fall for a smokejumper. Well, at least now, right?" She winked, pulling a towel from a stash in her locker. "I conveniently left out your wild high school years."

"What wild high school years?"

"Just because you were in love with only *one* hotshot didn't mean it wasn't wild," Gilly said. "Just you trying to get Jed's attention had my dad pacing the floor. Poor man paid the price for being your dad's best friend—it wasn't fair that Jock left him in charge of you whenever he had to leave town."

Kate finger-combed her hair out then pulled it back into a rough braid. "I wasn't trying to get Jed's attention."

"Lie to yourself if you want, but I know Jed Ransom's been on your radar since he landed on your doorstep when you were fifteen."

Gilly threw the towel over her shoulder. "Now comes the fun—you get to work with him. Boy howdy, I can't wait to see round two."

"He tried to fire me." Kate tugged on her T-shirt.

"What? He can't fire you. You're the jump trainer—"

"He's the supervisor. He *can* fire me, at least from the training crew. Apparently he thinks I'm a bad influence."

Gilly raised an eyebrow. "And...?"

"Stop. I'm the only one around here who's jumped into every terrain in North America. I've logged more jumps than Reuben, Conner, and Pete combined—and Jed hasn't even jumped since..."

Oh. Maybe Gilly didn't know about that, because she was staring at Kate with her eyes wide, all ears, so to speak.

"Miles knows I'm the most qualified. Jed can teach them fire tactics, sure, but I'm here to make sure they survive the fall. Or I was. Now I guess I'll throw my duffel bag back into Dad's truck and...I dunno. See if Missoula has any openings." Because she couldn't rightly return to Boise and the Inter-Departmental Fire Agency, could she? Not after her resounding exit, her declaration that Blazin' Kate Burns was *back,* jumping fire.

Of all her stupid moments, perhaps that was second only to today's.

"Besides, I'm over Jed Ransom. I promise."

Gilly took a breath, sat on the bench, holding her shampoo. "Whatever. But you're not going to let him run you off, are you? This is your hometown. You are Jock Burns's daughter. And frankly, this town needs you." Her voice turned somber. "There are a lot of people really hurting—we all are. We're a family here, and to lose seven of us—sure, three of the guys were from out of town, but you grew up with Nutter Turnquist. And Tommy Browning. And remember Bo Renner? He played running back for the Ember Flames."

Kate knew the names, of course, but hadn't spent any time putting faces to them. She sank onto the bench.

"Jock had charisma," Gilly said. "He inspired people and made them believe that what we did mattered. Suddenly people are asking themselves, why we are risking our lives for a chunk of land and property?"

"It's not about land and property—"

"It's about people. Exactly. And the fact that if we let fire blaze, suddenly neighborhoods get destroyed, and yes, people get killed. And that's what Jock would say. But now people aren't sure—and they're afraid. There's talk about shutting down the smokejumper team."

The team her father started so many years ago.

The team he had refused to let her be a part of.

The team that just might help her find her courage again.

"I told Jed that by the end of the summer I'd prove to him he needs me."

Gilly stood up. "Good. Because he needs you *now*, Kate. Always has, since the day he walked onto the Ember base. He just can't find the guts to admit it."

Which was why her walking away was for the best. Especially with him looking even more devastating than he had seven years ago. Blue eyes, dark hair cut short, slightly curly, the smattering of dark whiskers across his square chin. If possible, his shoulders seemed even more sculpted—all those years swinging a Pulaski—his waist lean and solid, his legs strong under those green Nomex pants. Sheesh, no wonder she'd harbored a decade-long crush on him—the man exuded an aura of strength that made her want to hold on.

But he'd burned her once—she didn't plan on diving back into the flames.

Gilly headed to the shower, and Kate finished dressing, grabbing a Jude County Wildland Firefighters hat for her wet head. She headed out of the bathroom and followed the laughter to the lounge.

Pete lay on the donated green sofa, tossing a football in the air. Reuben sat in an overstuffed chair, reaching for a slice of pizza. A couple of younger fellas—probably recruits— played a game on the Xbox, something with guns and fire and aliens.

The one wearing a cowboy hat, his blond hair curly out the back, glanced at her and nodded, using his manners. "Ma'am."

Oh for crying out loud. "Call me Kate."

"CJ St. John." He held out his hand, and she met his grip, found it chapped and worn from hard work.

Pete cocked his head toward the open door to the ready room. "Shh. We're listening to Conner and the boss have it out."

Sure enough, she heard voices.

Loud, angry voices. Pete sat up, took his feet off the sofa, patting the cushion.

Instead she held out her hands and he tossed her the football. She caught it. Rolled it in her grip.

"I have twenty-four recruits out there all hoping to land a spot on a team that the Forest Service isn't sure they want to continue. You know what will happen to this program if we have even one serious injury this summer?" Jed, his voice tight, dark.

"It's not if a jumper gets hurt—it's *when*." Conner's quiet, brutal addition.

She winced, knowing Conner's words had to hurt.

Silence.

She glanced at Pete, who shrugged, then Reuben, his mouth set in a grim line. It was true, however—smokejumping was listed among the twenty-five most dangerous jobs in the world. If jumpers didn't crash into trees, they could get blown into the fire, get injured by equipment, crushed by a falling snag, and, in the worst of scenarios, find themselves trapped by fire.

Finally, "Jumpers get hurt—that's to be expected. But we can't lose another life to fire."

Almost on reflex Kate's gaze went to the pictures of the seven, each memorialized in frames on the wall. Her dad's visage—clean shaven, wearing his Forest Service uniform— grinned out at her, and she looked away before her throat tightened.

But nothing braced her for Jed's next words. "Kate is as reckless as they come. You've heard the stories—"

"I have." This from Pete. "They're pretty amazing. I heard you outran a bear!"

Every gaze landed on her.

"It was a cub," she muttered under the heated voices in the next room.

"Sure, she takes risks, but she's got a reputation for knowing how a fire behaves," Conner was saying. "And for reacting fast. Pete's not the first jumper she's saved out of the sky—"

"I'm a little brokenhearted," Pete said frowning at her. "Already stepping out on me?"

"What can I say?" Kate said, but Jed's words overran her, left her shaken.

"Believe me, I know every single one of Kate's exploits."

He did? She swallowed, felt the blood drain from her face.

But her eyes closed against his next words.

"Taking risks doesn't have to include being reckless. And Blazin' Kate is the poster child for reckless. She's going to get people hurt trying to prove she's just as good as her father."

And that was her cue. "I'm outta here."

"He doesn't mean it—" Pete started, but she held up her hand.

"Oh, yes he does." She tossed him the ball.

Pete was on his feet, wearing a pained expression. "Kate—"

She couldn't take the way he was looking at her, Jed's words adding pity to his expression. So, "Before you get ambitious, Pete, I don't date smokejumpers."

A second, a beat, and then he rebounded, saving her. "There you go, breaking my heart again." He even put his hands over his chest.

She grinned and shook her head against the laughter of the team. But Jed's words burned inside her.

She's going to get people hurt.

Not this time.

Jed should have known that Conner, former Green Beret and the team's communication expert, would track him down, attempt to talk him out of the rash decision to fire the team's new trainer.

He just hadn't expected it to happen in the middle of Overhead, around listening ears.

"Jed, take a beat here. Think about this."

Conner didn't do anything rash. Ever. And, frankly, neither did Jed.

Unless, of course, Kate Burns walked into his airspace. Which was exactly why he'd had to fire her from the training crew. And why he didn't even want her jumping.

He cut his voice to low. "Trust me on this—Kate is trouble."

"You can't just fire her—"

"Yes, I can," Jed had said, not stopping to have it out with Conner. Not when he couldn't catch a full breath. "I can't believe the entire town of Ember applauded her. Do they have any idea what that does to morale? Now every recruit will be dreaming of becoming a daredevil in the sky."

He turned then and headed for the smokejumper wing, located right across the hall from the Jude County Wildland Firefighters offices.

"She's Jock Burns's daughter!"

"I know. Believe me, *I know*."

Their fight echoed in his head as he passed the locker room. *Not on my watch. Somebody has to keep you from fulfilling your death wish. Like father, like daughter.*

He shouldn't have said that—his hurt, his grief emerging in accusation.

He glanced at Conner, who'd dropped his gear on the floor of the locker room, scrambling behind him.

"This is Jock's fault," Jed said. "He always fed her stories of his crazy jumps and conveniently forgot the parts where he nearly got skewered by a tree or torched by some falling snag or some errant breeze that set him down in the middle of an inferno. She grew up thinking he was invincible."

Jed stood for a moment in the middle of the ready room, tasting the rampage of his heart in his throat. Buffalo, moose, and elk heads peered over the expanse, and at the front of the room chairs scattered a loose semicircle in front of a white board, the roster list, a call-out activity board, and eight-by-tens of every Jock Burns Jude County smokejumping crew since the man began the team some twenty years ago.

Talk about legacy.

"You can't fire her for saving Pete's life."

"And I'm not firing her for saving Pete's life. I'm firing her because..." He shook his head. "Because this town has had enough death."

He couldn't be here.

Jed took a breath and headed past the rigging area, the four long parachute-folding tables near the back of the room, past the Singer sewing machines and a utility table cluttered with irons, tape, rolls of cord, and material, straight for the three-story tower where they hung the parachutes. He didn't know why, exactly, standing amid the silky clouds calmed him, but he found himself pacing through the folds of white, creamy fabric.

Putting himself back together.

CHAPTER 3

N O ONE BUT KATE BURNS could push him past himself, ignite a side to him he wanted to extinguish.

He let the silk slide through his hands.

He shook his head. "I've been fighting fires since I was seventeen, and I can't remember being this rattled."

Oh. He didn't exactly mean to say that out loud, and now glanced behind him, hoping he hadn't.

Conner was looking at him, his expression enigmatic.

"I've never lost a firefighter," Jed said.

"I know," Conner said quietly. "That's why they chose you to take Jock's place."

Jed let go of the silk. "They called Jock Mr. Bad Decision, Good Outcome. Did you know that?"

Conner made a noise of agreement behind him.

"I don't have that kind of luck."

Jed closed his eyes, listening to the hammer of his heart, finally slowing, then took a breath and brushed past Conner, heading for the roster board at the front of the room. Just outside, in the lounge, Jed heard laughter, smelled pizza—someone had reheated yesterday's lunch.

He wanted to join them, but how could he, with the

weight of their futures in his hands?

Jed stared at the board, first at his slim roster of veterans, then at the twenty-four pictures of every single recruit, along with their names and states of origin tacked on the wall. "I know their names. Their hometowns. How long they've been hotshots. I have a pretty good idea of whether they'll make it or not. But more importantly, I have to keep them alive. Just like Jock did."

He walked over to one of the pictures, a crew shot taken nine years ago. He recognized himself, young, bright-eyed, wearing his gear, two weeks of grizzle on his chin, grinning as if he owned the world.

Back then, he had. That picture had been taken just after he'd returned from a tour in Idaho. He distinctly remembered being on his way to the Hotline later that night, hoping to bump into Kate.

"You will, Jed." Conner walked up to him. Peered at a more recent picture of himself. "Wow, I needed a haircut."

"You still do."

"Kate's not in any of these pictures."

No, she wasn't. Thankfully. "Jock didn't let her jump for his crew."

"Why not?"

For the same reason Jed couldn't. "He couldn't bear it if she got hurt on his watch."

Conner fell silent. Then, "I think she deserves a chance to prove herself—not that she already hasn't."

Jed glanced at the pictures of the last crew—Tommy, Bo, Nutter. Jock's square-chinned, dirty, handsome face grinned at him from the middle of the group, and a fist squeezed in his chest. He hadn't expected to miss the guy this much, even ten months later.

The truth was, Kate could jump every bit as well as her father. The problem was that Jed couldn't think straight with Kate in his radar. He'd nearly gotten them killed trying to prove otherwise.

He walked over to the window, stared out at the tarmac, at the planes.

"Jock was like a father to me. I can hardly breathe thinking about how he died. He was the one who got me into firefighting, taught me everything I know. I can't believe it's up to me to fill his shoes."

He sighed, turned to Conner. "But that's my job—and if I don't figure out a way to bring this team—and this town—together by the end of the summer, then Jock Burns's legacy will die with him." He shook his head. "And I can't let anything—even his daughter—stand in the way. This town needs a victory, healing. Peace. And the only way they're going to have peace is if they know they're safe."

Conner sighed. "If she doesn't train them, who will?"

"Me. I've trained jumpers before—in Alaska."

And this time he'd do it right.

How Kate had missed the easy, sweetly numbing atmosphere of Friday nights at the Ember Hotline Saloon and Grill.

The redolence of memory embedded the walls, from the greasy tang of bar food—burgers, O-rings, and chili fries—to the twang of the music from the ancient Wurlitzer near the dance floor. Someone had chosen a one-hit wonder. *Lay down that boogie and play that Funky Music till you die...*

Pictures of every Jude County hotshot team for the past twenty years hung in eight-by-tens covering every available space on the pine-slabbed walls, along with the tools of the trade—Pulaskis, orange hard hats, and not a few autographs from former Strike Team leaders.

With another fire season simmering just across the horizon, the fresh recruits assembled in groups throughout the room, raucous and looking for a fight with the powers of nature. Meanwhile, veteran hotshots, fresh in from their winter jobs, jammed onto picnic tables shoved in the middle of the room. They drank microbrews, wolfed down Juicy Lucy burgers, and sopped curly fries through the signature Hotline concoction of mayo, chili-sauce, and fresh jalapenos.

Kate sat on a high top at the bar, nursing a malt.

After a week of refresher training, the team of veteran jumpers formed their own motley crew near the dartboard in back. A crew rife with comments on the fate of the rookies.

"Those two skinny kids will be crying for their momma the minute they see a real fire. Ten bucks says they cut and run before the final march," Pete said, gesturing to a pair of preppy, skinny high school graduates, eyes eager for adventure. Kate had seen the type and agreed. They didn't have the look.

"How about those yahoos," Reuben said. "They're sitting with my cousin Ned from Minnesota."

Kate spotted Ned easily—younger than Reuben by a few years, he bore the handsome, rangy looks of his cousin, with the dark brown eyes and dark brown curly hair. Of the other two, one wore his dark-as-night hair long, curly, pulled back in a knot and bore the look of someone who knew his way around trouble. Tucker Newman, also from Minnesota, if she remembered the list correctly.

"The tough one—he looks like a snowboarder filling in for the off-season," Reuben said. "The other—CJ—he's Montana ranch boy all the way."

CJ ate his fries, eyes down, wearing a Stetson, his dark blond hair hinting out from the back. His black T-shirt bunched around his biceps, either a bruise or a tattoo peeking out on the upper arm. Yeah, he had rodeo written all over him.

"His uncle Rafe used to ride bulls professionally," Reuben added, eyeing the bull's-eye before letting a dart fly.

Gilly Priest came sauntering into the bar and slid on a stool. Their pilot had shed her usual aviator shades and JCWF hat in favor of a black tank and a pair of jeans. Petite and tough, Gilly considered herself part of the team—and rightly so. Enough to keep a cool distance from the guys during her off-hours. Kate noticed, however, Reuben's eyes trail over her a moment longer than he might for, say, Pete.

Oh, Reuben. Kate longed to warn him off. Gilly, too, had grown up in Ember and knew better than to fall for smoke-jumpers. Especially the brooding tough guys who had a story behind their devastating blue eyes.

"I think 'Bambi' over there is going to fall asleep in her hamburger," Gilly said.

Kate followed Gilly's gesture to one of the few female recruits, curvy, but with enough muscle on her to survive. Maybe. 'Bambi's' head rested on her hand, eyes closed, her other hand wrapped around her half-eaten bison burger. Dressed in clean green pants and a T-shirt, her brown hair pulled back in a braid, the girl looked as if she'd just trekked in after a ten-mile hike with a full pack.

"That's Hannah Butcher," Kate said.

"Oh, right," Gilly said. "Her sister was married to Nutter."

A moment of silence while everyone settled into comprehension. A local girl picking up the family mantle.

"I remember being that exhausted after my first week in rookie training." Kate said, taking another sip of her malt.

"I dunno," Pete said, leaning against the bar. "Jed's training them like a man possessed. Two workouts every day, spot tests on the classroom lessons, and I swear they've run to the border and back. Today they did their first ninety-minute march, full packs. Three bailed after an hour. I don't know how the rest did—I couldn't watch."

She could. In fact, after she'd finished her own workout, showered, and taken a quick stop at Overhead to check out the conditions, she'd driven up to her father's old Airstream camper, located on a bluff overlooking the fire camp, to watch the fun.

"Five more dropped out by the end," she said. "And Jed's not giving second chances."

"Ouch," Reuben said from his position by the dartboard. "At this rate, we'll have a skeleton crew."

Exactly. Kate knew the brutal pain of lugging one hundred pounds for three miles and didn't envy the trainees, especially in the extraordinary ninety-degree heat that turned their Montana base into a fry pan.

But she might have doused them with cold water, shoved them into the truck, and given them a second chance instead of handing them their walking papers. If she remembered right, she hadn't made that first march either.

"I can't believe bruiser over there didn't make it," Conner said, gesturing to a large dark-haired bull of a man in the corner. "He's a sawyer for the Redding Shots, name's Gary." The big man sat alone at a table in the corner, silent, nursing a brew, another glass empty, his chili fries mostly uneaten. He stared vacantly out the window, as if stunned.

Well, Jed did that to a person. Left their head spinning and their hopes decimated.

Blazin' Kate is the poster child for risk. She's going to get people hurt trying to prove that she's just as good as her father.

His words had twisted through her brain all week, from her up-at-dawn eight-mile run through PT with the team. It poked at her through their refresher training on landing rolls, letdowns, suit-up practice, and emergency aircraft techniques. She'd mulled it through even as she hung out in the loft repairing parachutes.

If anyone were trying to prove himself, it was Jed.

"I still don't understand why Jed got so lathered up when you saved Pete's life," Gilly said, turning to Kate. "Pete would have made an ugly smear all over our pretty landing zone."

"Hey." But Pete grinned and glanced at Kate. "She's my hero."

"You would have done the same thing," she said. "We got lucky."

"Anytime you need saving, I'm your man." Pete winked and walked over to Reuben.

Gilly's gaze followed him, then landed on Reuben. Oh, well then...

In a second she returned it to Kate and cut her voice low. "So, listen. I know you and I know Jed, and I've been thinking about the most recent Great Fight and your assertion that you're 'over' him." Gilly added finger quotes for emphasis. "And I think you're not coming clean with your BFF." She leaned in close, her blue eyes shining. "What aren't you telling me? After all those years of batting your eyes at Big Jed Ransom, something happened that you're not telling me, didn't it?"

And just like that, heat rushed to Kate's face, betraying her.

Gilly leaned back, mouth agape. "No—"

"Shh. It wasn't like that. We...nothing happened. Not really."

"Please. I can't remember a day when you didn't pine for
Jed Ransom, not since the day he showed up and your daddy
decided to make him his protégé."

"Dad liked him way too much," Kate said, her mind so
easily conjuring up Jed as a lanky, broad-shouldered seventeen-year-old, dark hair combed Elvis style, wide-eyed and
eager to make the Jude County hotshot team. He'd shown
up on the doorstep of the Airstream, looking for Jock Burns,
and when he found him, stuck to him like he wanted to be
adopted.

"He was always a little overprotective of you. Poor Jed
probably thought he was your brother instead of a hot male
in the company of a girl who wanted to give him her heart.
Either that or Jock threatened his life if he even looked at you
with anything but a protective eye."

Kate nodded, the memories sweet. "Remember that time
he took my dad's pickup?"

"When Jed tracked us down fifteen miles into the Kootenai? Oh, he was steamed. He'd just come back from some
big fire in Alaska, and he acted like you were supposed to be
waiting for him. As if."

Kate offered a weak smile. *As if.* Miraculously, she managed to tame the memories before they surfaced. The feel of
Jed's hand on the small of her back, the other on her cheek,
the look in his devastating eyes when his gaze traced her face.

The feel of his mouth brushing her skin.

I never blamed you.

Oh, yes he did.

She took a sip of her malt, let the chill into her bones.

"Well, I think he might regret panicking and accusing
you of tainting the rookies with your sense of epic heroism."
Gilly glanced around the room at the tired, despondent re-

cruits. "I think they might need a healthy dose."

The music changed to the Jackson 5, "I Want You Back." *Oh baby all I need is one more chance.*

"And oh my, look who just walked in." Gilly nodded toward the door just as Jed stepped inside.

He hadn't shaved, giving himself over to a smattering of dark whiskers across his chin, but looked freshly showered, his hair shiny and slicked back, wearing a crisp white T-shirt and faded jeans, flip-flops. He shoved his hands into his pockets, his jaw tight as he surveyed the room, apparently friendless.

"Invite him over here," Gilly said.

"No—"

But her heart went out to him just a smidgen when she saw him slide onto a high-top chair, away from the crowd.

Stay out of my way.

"We nearly died together."

She didn't know why—or how—the words slipped out. But seeing him sitting there, his biceps stretching the sleeves of his shirt, looking worn and not a little lonely, she could practically feel him tremble in her arms despite the courage he'd attempted in his voice. *We're going to live, Kate, I promise.*

"What—?" Gilly cut through her memory. "Did you say you nearly *died* together?"

Kate played with the straw in her malt. Nodded. "It was my rookie year, up in Alaska."

"Oh, I remember. Jock was so angry when you joined the Midnight Sun Jumpers."

"Little did I know that Jed was on the team."

Gilly's eyes widened. "What? Why did you never tell me?"

Kate looked away.

"Oh, Kate." Gilly slid her hand to touch Kate's arm.

"What happened?"

She didn't know where to start. Looked at Jed.

He picked at his curly fries. Had barely touched his beer, now sweating on the counter.

We danced. We kissed. And then he nearly died trying to save my life.

"About my fifth jump of the season, we were called in to knock down a fire on the Porcupine River, north of the Yukon. Jed was my jump partner."

She saw it then, about two acres of flame crawling toward higher land. Their LZ—landing zone—surrounded by tall pines and huge boulders and, of course, the river. The tunnel of smoke to the east, the smell of smoke faint, a hint of danger.

"I jumped before he did. About a quarter mile down, as I came into the canyon, a wind shear rushed up and practically threw me over the ridge into the fire. I stalled, then managed to refill. I somehow steered away from the fire, but I messed up—I overcorrected and came down a good three miles from the drop zone. In a small clearing surrounded by pine."

"I put down and rolled—a clean landing, but when I came up, I heard someone shouting. Jed—snagged in a tree."

"He came after you."

"Yeah. He thought I was in trouble, off course, and decided to follow me. But then he came down hard into the trees and his leg got caught on a limb. Not a compound, but a fracture all the same. He was able to let down, but he could barely walk. We called for a pickup, but we were short a chopper, and the jumpers couldn't cross the ridge. We were cut off. And right in the path of the fire."

"No one can read a fire like Jed." This from Pete. She hadn't seen him sidle up next to her, his head on his hand, leaning into the story. Reuben, too, stood nearby, now holding a pool cue, chalking it over and over.

She wasn't sure, then, how much of this story she should tell and shot a glance at Jed. He simply stared at the mirror behind the bar, as if reliving the story with her. Except, in the crowded bar, he couldn't exactly hear her, right?

"We got trapped. And I..." She shook her head. "Anyway, Jed grabbed me and threw me to the ground, shook out my shelter over me. I was climbing in when I realized—with his fractured leg there was no way he could keep his shelter secure. So I climbed in with him, helped him hold his shelter down."

"You rode through a fire—in the same shelter?" Gilly asked, her voice betraying exactly how Kate felt about it.

Kate nodded.

"You saved his life."

She shook her head, ran her finger down the moisture on the side of the glass. "Nope. The thing was, I was pretty freaked out. And I'm not sure if I wouldn't have simply gotten up to run if he wasn't holding me down. He saved *my* life."

The team fell quiet, Pete glancing to Jed. Gilly played with the edge of her napkin.

And there was no need to tell them the rest, because maybe they got it. You didn't go through something like that with someone and not emerge bonded.

"No wonder he freaked out when you came after me," Pete said quietly. "The guy is in love with you."

Kate stared at him, her mouth open. "What—how—did you hear him? He practically took off my head."

"I know," Pete said, grinning.

"Trust me. He's not in love with me."

"A girl saves my backside, I love her a little bit," Pete said. "Or a lot."

"Don't go dropping to your knees, Brooks."

Shouting from the front of the saloon diverted Pete's response. She turned and spotted Gary, the buffalo, rising from the table. His chair toppled over, hit the floor with a bang. He shouted again, more clearly. "Ransom, who do you think you are?"

Jed didn't move.

Gary bullied his way past a couple of rookies who stood in his path, pressing their hands to his chest. "I'm talking to you, Ransom!"

Jed just kept staring straight ahead.

Next to Kate, Pete put down his drink.

Reuben pocketed the chalk, his grip curling around the pool cue.

Two men had the sawyer by the arms, but he pushed one away, and the man landed hard on the wood floor. Chairs squealed back, voices shouted, but Gary kept going.

Kate found her feet, her heart lodged in her ribs as the bar fell into a hush.

Even in a crowded bar, with his recruits and veterans huddled over in private gripe sessions about their new boss, Jed knew Kate had been talking.

About him.

He'd noticed her sitting on a stool in the back of the bar the minute he walked in. She always possessed a sort of magnetic ability to arrest his attention, stop his heartbeat for a moment, and his gaze found her even now as she nursed—of course—a chocolate malt, her dark red hair loose around her shoulders, framing her beautiful face, those gray-green eyes, her curves outlined in a blue Jude County Wildland Firefighters T-shirt.

He couldn't make out her words, but he read her story in the way she kept glancing at him and using her hands. And he braced himself for the moment when she'd get to the part where he'd lost it, nearly came unglued as the Porcupine River fire tried to deep-fry them. Or maybe the part afterwards, when his wounds caused him to go into shock.

Hopefully, however, she'd pulled back from revealing that moment in the hospital when he'd turned into a coward.

"I'm talking to you, Ransom!"

Jed hadn't even heard the man until the bar quieted, until the voice, slurred and bitter, saturated the room.

He didn't move. Just watched in the mirror as Gary approached him. Oh, he'd made a wise decision when he cut Big Gare from the squad.

Now, he had two choices, and he contemplated them in a long, protracted second as Gary's sweaty mitt landed on his shoulder. Turn fast and sink his fist into Gary's face, send him sprawling and remind him exactly who was in charge. Or... Jed could do what Jock had taught him.

Take a breath. Think. Find the contingencies, keep his feet under him.

The first choice spoke to the restless, angry energy prowling around inside him for a week now. And especially today when he was down to twelve of his twenty-four recruits. *Twelve.* This season's rookie class might be decimated before the season even began.

Tackling Gary and letting his anger, his frustration loose on the man would only sabotage morale. With last year's tragedy looming over the fire base, his crew needed to trust him. Which meant he needed to earn their respect.

Jed took a breath and slid off the stool.

Gary appeared ready to take off his head, his eyes glassy, his words sloppy, so Jed kept it simple.

"Step back, Gary. This isn't going to help."

Around the room, recruits and veterans bounced to their feet—in whose corner he didn't want to guess. He glanced past Gary, saw the booth of rookie smokejumper recruits— CJ St. John, Tucker Newman, and Ned Marshall—spilling out. CJ adjusted his cowboy hat while Tucker assessed the situation with what seemed like practiced eyes.

Out of his peripheral vision, Jed spotted Kate, stanchioned by Pete and Reuben, working her way down the bar.

Stay outta this, Kate. But that thought was pure reflex as Gary's mouth tipped in a drunken smile.

It almost wasn't fair. Because Jed had grown up with a brother five years older, bigger and faster, who thought Jed should learn how to take care of himself should their uncle ever, finally, kick them out. And Abe wasn't one to pull his punches.

Gary's beefy fist came at him what felt like in slow motion, and Jed moved so fast he almost had to wait for the man to fly past him. He stepped aside and let Gary's momentum do the work. Gary slammed hard into the bar, bounced back and, aided by his copious refills of the special on tap, stepped back, woozy.

Jed grabbed his shirt. "Are you finished?"

Apparently not, because Gary swung again. Jed ducked and reluctantly grabbed his shoulder, loaded a punch into his gut that had Gary doubling over.

Jed directed him to collapse in a chair as the man turned

green. "Sit there. Sober up. Go home."

The bar remained quiet, and even Kate stopped walking his direction. He looked up at the expressions of his audience, more than a few wide-eyed.

CJ nodded to him, touching the brim of his hat. Tucker gave him a half grin and slid back into his booth.

A couple of the recruits he'd cut came over, eyed him, and picked up Gary, disoriented and grousing, but the fight blown out of him.

Only then did Jed feel the adrenaline sluice through him. It turned him edgy, his stomach clenching. As the crowd turned back to their dinners, he braced a hand on the bar. He might have worked harder this week than he thought, running alongside the recruits, leading them in PT, showing them the proper tuck and roll for a landing, then staying up late to read weather reports and check in with Conner, who was working with the veterans, helping with the refresher course.

He sank onto the stool, closed his eyes against the spin in the room.

"Can we get this to go?"

Kate. He looked up to find her standing next to him, holding out his curly fries to the bartender. Up close she smelled good, her hair soft around her shoulders.

"I'm not—"

"Yes you are."

Hungry, was what he was going to say, but maybe it didn't matter, because whatever he said, she was going to argue.

And suddenly he didn't have the energy to fight with her, at least not tonight.

"Did you drive?" she said, apparently looking for his keys.

"They're in the bike."

She took the box of curly fries. "Add it to my tab, Patrice."

He thought the bartender looked familiar but could barely make out the likeness behind the midnight-black dyed hair and gauged ears. And she might have lost about thirty pounds.

Aged a few years past high school.

"Are you Bo Renner's sister?" he asked as Kate got him up.

"Yes," Kate answered for her. "C'mon, let's get out of here."

He cut his words off then, seeing how Patrice looked at him, grief in her eyes.

"I'm sorry," he said softly, not sure Patrice even heard him as he let Kate lead him to the door.

Dust settled over the town of Ember, a simmering orange just rimming the mountains to the west, and a cool, piney breeze picked up, tempering the heat of the day.

"I can smell rain," Kate said. She still had a steadying, bossy grip on his arm, and he let it stay.

Just for now.

"It hasn't rained yet this season," he said. In fact, the tinder was so dry the Forest Service had already outlawed campfires in the park.

"It might be too high up, but we're definitely in for a thunderstorm."

"Which means lightning," he said as he followed her to his bike. "You always did have Jock's weather instincts."

Oh, he didn't know why he said that—maybe a peace offering.

She didn't look at him in reproach or assent, just picked

up the helmet. Handed it to him.

He expected her to leave him then, having prodded him out of the bar. Instead she took the key and opened the seat box. "Don't you keep a second helmet in here?"

Before he could answer, she found it and pried it out. She put the box of curly fries inside, then snapped on the helmet and turned to him. "You're on the back."

She—huh? But she didn't wait for him, just threw her leg over the seat and leveraged the bike off the kickstand. Then, "Getting on?"

"I can get the bike home, Kate."

"I know. But you're tired and drank half your beer, and frankly, that fight in there is my fault. Besides, you know I've always wanted to ride your bike."

And for a second, everything dropped away—their fight from a week ago, seven years of tangled emotions, even the searing regret of the mistakes that nearly took their lives. Just Kate, smiling at him as if there might be hope for a fragile friendship.

Huh. He stood there a moment, debating, wondering just how many of his recruits might be watching.

"C'mon, Jed. This isn't a fire. You can trust me to get you home." And, for a second, hurt shone in her eyes behind the soft smile.

"I know," he said. He sat behind her, settling his hands on her hips. "When did you learn how to ride a bike?"

"Rudy taught me."

One of the rookie jumpers who'd lasted through the Alaska summer, sticking around after Jed had walked away—or rather, limped away on crutches, back to the lower forty-eight.

She took off down the single road that cut through Ember. Stopping at the only light in town, she flicked on the radio. Ember's KFire filled the air with a Boston tune—oldies night.

It's more than a feeling...

Oh, that wasn't fair. His heartbeat slowed with the easiness of letting her drive, moving in tune with her as she turned left, toward the fire base.

He couldn't help the longing to move his hands up, touch her shoulders, her arms. To draw her back against himself.

Wow, this was a bad idea. The sense of her under his hands roused the memories, and he was powerless to fight them.

I...dream of a girl I used to know...I closed my eyes and she slipped away...

"This song was playing that night I showed up in Alaska. I still remember it."

She glanced over her shoulder at him, her visor up. "I remember that. We were still putting the station together for the season—the place was a mess. There were guys sewing chutes, and I was working on inventory. I couldn't believe it when you walked in."

What are you doing here?

The surprise in her voice, the wide-eyed, masked expression—sometimes the guilt could still rise from the dead to choke him.

"I just remember you smelled like something that lived under a Dumpster," she said.

"Oh, that's real nice, Kate. I *had* been on the road for five days."

"You looked like it, too—greasy hair, unshaven. And I admit, for a minute there, I thought Dad had sent you."

He swallowed hard, her words a knife, but thankfully she

looked back and gunned the bike.

Just go up there, and make sure she quits.

Hardly. Jock clearly didn't know his daughter like Jed did. But he'd owed Jock so much, he couldn't say no. Until, of course, Jed betrayed him.

And nearly cost Kate her life.

Jed leaned with her as they turned onto the dirt road that led past the base, the meadow where they practiced their landings, then the jump platform, and in the distance, the barracks, the mess hall, the Overhead office. To the east, Glacier National Park rose dark and foreboding.

Kate was taking him to Jock's place.

She turned onto the rutted, grassy road that edged her into Jock's acreage, and he spotted the camper, permanently parked on a bluff overlooking the fire camp. It gleamed in the moonlight. They pulled up in back onto the parking pad and she held the bike as he climbed off.

Setting her helmet on the seat, she said, "C'mon. I need to give you something."

She didn't wait for him but walked up the path, flicking on the string of Christmas lights that framed the deck, freshly built last summer on Jock's off days. "Wait here," she said, and he settled down at the picnic table while she went inside.

Music drifted out from the kitchen, more oldies from KFire.

Why do you build me up, Buttercup...

He held his head in his hand, listening to his thundering heartbeat, not sure how he got here.

"I found this in Dad's stuff. I thought you'd like it." She came out, climbed over the bench opposite him, and handed him a picture frame.

He stared at it in the fading light, recognition closing over him, a fist in his chest. A cut-out newspaper picture. Jock, his face blackened, reverse raccoon eyes, leaning on his Pulaski, and next to him, looking identical, nearly father and son, Jed.

"The *Ember Torch* took this picture of us that first year I made it on the jump team. We'd just knocked down the Camp Creek fire."

"I remember," Kate said quietly. "I was a senior in high school, and it was the first summer Dad let me work a fire. You probably don't remember, but I was on that crew with you—"

"I remember." He looked up at her, met her eyes.

She blinked, then a half smile tugged up her face. "Right. Well, anyway, I thought you'd like to have that."

She got up then and walked over to a cooler, opened it, and pulled out two dripping bottles of lemonade.

Handed him one.

He took his, popped open the top, then exchanged it for hers, popped that. Held it up and she tapped it. "To Jock."

"And the job he loved." She took a sip, then, to his surprise, climbed up on the picnic table and leaned back, lying along the length of it, staring at the sky.

"Remember that night we jumped into Copper Canyon?" she said. "It was my first real jump, and it was so weird to see the aurora borealis backdropped by all that fire and smoke. Green and red mixed with silver and black. Surreal."

He wanted to climb up, tuck himself in beside her, and the urge felt so powerful it shook through him. But he couldn't. Never again, and especially not sitting here, at Jock's place—the man's voice practically inhabiting his head.

I'm trusting her to you, Jed.

Right.

Instead, Jed lay down on the bench below her. Overhead the stars fought to pierce the cloud cover, the Milky Way muted.

"I wish you'd been there, with him."

Her words jolted him, but he knew, exactly what she meant.

"Me too—"

"Not that I would have wanted—" She rolled over and peered down at him, her eyes wide. "I didn't mean—"

"I know, Kate. I wish I had been there, too. I should have stayed in the field."

"You had no choice—they pulled you out." She rolled back over, vanished from his sight.

Maybe. It didn't stop the voices.

He finally sat up, took a sip of the lemonade, picked at the label, trying to find the right words. "I've read the reports and...it was just a fluke blowup. The wind shifted, it was blowing over forty miles an hour, and the fire just turned on them. Flame lengths were over three hundred feet, and it ran a mile in three minutes—"

"And Dad was in the safety zone. He should have stayed put. But he turned around and ran right into the fire." She sat up now, too, and when he looked at her, her eyes glistened.

Oh, Kate.

He knew the nightmares, the questions in her expression. He, too, wanted to crawl inside Jock's brain.

The man was a forty-year veteran, had lived through countless blowups, including taking cover in a fire shelter at least three times in his career.

And yet—

The worst part was, if Jock Burns could screw up, make a mistake that cost people their lives, what kept Jed from doing the same?

"I don't understand why he did what he did," Kate said softly. She, too, thumbed the soggy label on her bottle. "And that is, actually, why I came back. Yeah, I have to pack up all of this, but I have to get my head around what happened and why. I think that's the only way I can say good-bye."

She closed her eyes, drew her knees up, wrapped her arms around them. Her breath came out shaky. "I wish I had come back sooner."

He had nothing for her then, because he agreed with her.

But it didn't mean that he didn't blame himself for the falling out that cost her and Jock so much.

"I'm sorry, Kate," he said finally. "I shouldn't have gotten so angry with you this week. I just—I know it's not fair, but it takes a little piece out of me every time you jump."

She looked away. Silence, except for the hum of the radio.

I-I-I need you-oo-oo more than anyone, baby...You know that I have from the start.

In the distance, thunder rolled.

"I think there'll be fire tonight," she said softly, before pressing the lemonade bottle to her lips. Her hair curled against her shoulders, her profile outlined by the twinkling lights, and inside he felt the stirring of everything he'd attempted to douse.

He couldn't agree more.

CHAPTER 4

KATE COULDN'T PUT WORDS to why she'd decided to tug Jed's arm, urge him out of the Hotline and onto his motorcycle. Why she didn't just send him home, or back to the fire camp, take her own Jeep to end the night staring at the stars.

Why she brought him up here, as if to retrace history.

Start over, maybe.

But sitting here with him touched a part of her that, ever since receiving the news about her dad, felt cracked and parched, as if thirsting for something that no amount of time could repair.

"Gary would have never made it, by the way," she said. "But you might consider going easier on your recruits. Give them more than a week to prove themselves."

She glanced over at Jed, at his dark profile, that strong jaw, his amazing shoulders. "You weren't so different, if I remember, when you showed up here, a skinny and starry-eyed teenager. You were driving that old Kawasaki. I loved that bike."

"I remember. You begged me constantly for a ride."

"Which you never gave me." She angled a look at him. "Well, until Alaska."

He looked down at his lemonade, and she suddenly had a glimpse of him seven years ago, waiting for her on his bike after Birch, their squad boss, had cut the rookies loose.

Or, she'd hoped he'd been waiting for her. Seated astride the bike, looking lean and strong in a pair of off-duty jeans, a white T-shirt under a flannel shirt rolled up past the elbows. He wore a baseball cap and his hair longer, behind his ears.

Same smoky blue eyes, however, and as she emerged from her quarters on the way to the chow hall, they dragged over her, a slow smile crawling up his face.

"Get on," he'd said. And without another thought, she did. Not that she hadn't seen Jed watching her during the two weeks of training, but she'd thought him unfazed by the fact they might spend the summer together, jumping, fighting fire.

Without her dad's gimlet eye on them.

Her wild fantasies had taken flight as she tucked herself behind him that night, her arms around his toned, washboard waist, softly inhaling his smell imbued sweetly with the scent of the Alaskan woods.

"I couldn't believe it," she said now, trying to tame her heartbeat. "Here I thought you were going to give me some amazing ride to the top of a mountain. Instead—"

"I bought you ice cream."

"Not until after you made me recite all the corrective actions for a chute failure."

He grinned, staring down, away from her, as if he, too, might be remembering their ride under the twilight sky, the way he'd curled his hand over her arms locked around his waist. "Drogue in tow," he said softly.

"Seriously?"

He glanced at her now, something of mischief in his eyes.

And a hint of dare.

"Fine. Cut away and deploy reserve."

"Horseshoe."

"Try and free it from your body. If not, then cut away and deploy reserve. Your turn. You're spinning."

"I'll say. What's in this lemonade?"

She wanted to reach out and give him a shove, the memory of sitting across from him slurping up a cone so powerful it could pull her under.

"Fine. Try and correct the spin. If no luck, cut away and deploy reserve."

She looked away, stared at the horizon where the mountains rose, humpbacked and black against the deep indigo of the evening. The wind stirred the string of lights she'd put up shortly after arriving.

"So why did it take you until Alaska to give me that ride?"

"One word, your guess."

She frowned, and he gave her a look like she should know this one.

"Dad?"

"First time you asked me for a ride, he cornered me in the loft and said that if I ever gave in, he'd send me packing."

Her mouth opened and she set down her lemonade. "And you let him bully you?"

His expression turned incredulous. "Of course I did. He was Jock Burns, and I was a punk seventeen-year-old kid with nowhere to go."

Oh. She didn't know that part. She scooted next to him, put her feet over the edge, propped her elbows on her knees. "I never did figure out—why my dad? You could have gone to the Missoula Base. Why did you track him down?"

"He never told you the story?"

She shook her head. "Maybe he thought it was only yours to tell."

Jed's mouth lifted. "I was fourteen, living with my uncle on a ranch just south of the park. The summer turned into a scorcher early in June, and by July the grass was brittle and some idiot in the park left his campfire smoldering. I'll never forget waking up to the smoke settling low in the valley. I couldn't see a thing except the flames in the distance. The thing was, my uncle had taken the truck into town the night before and didn't come home. I was trapped there—until suddenly, right out of the smoke, like some kind of super-hero, here comes your dad. He's sooty and tired and carrying a chainsaw over his shoulder, packing out with his team of jumpers who had just cut line across the edge of the pasture. He takes one look at me and realizes I'm alone and takes me along to their pickup spot. And all along the way, I'm peppering him with questions and he's answering them, one at a time in that calm, cool voice of his, not a hint that I might be annoying him." Jed took a breath then, and Kate knew he was comparing her dad to his uncle and his old man, to her knowledge still sitting in jail for armed burglary.

"By the time we found the hotshots, I knew I wanted to fight fire." He looked up at her. "Be the kind of man who keeps people calm, who knows how to soothe fears."

You are that kind of man. The words simmered inside her. Or at least he had been.

"I can't believe Dad had that kind of pull over your life."

"I owed him my entire career. He taught me everything. I would have done anything for him. And he would have done anything for you." He paused then, and the hesitation made her glance over, frown at the texture of guilt on his face.

"What?"

He took a breath, then, "He's the one who sent me to Alaska that summer. I didn't just show up there randomly."

She stilled. Put down her lemonade. "What?"

He gave her what looked like chagrin. "He wasn't thrilled—especially after keeping you off the team in Ember. So he asked me to keep an eye on you and..."

The realization came to her as his words trailed off, the expression of guilt cresting over his face.

No. But it suddenly made perfect, crystal-clear sense. "I always wondered why you got transferred to the team in Alaska. It was Dad—he pulled strings and sent you there. Because he wanted you to protect me, didn't he?"

"Something like that." His mouth lifted up on one side.

Oh. Wait. "No. He didn't want me to jump fire. He wanted—" She swallowed. "Did he send you up there to make sure I failed?"

"Kate, don't get upset—"

"Don't get *upset*? My father wanted you to sabotage me, and you went along with it?"

Jed looked stricken. "No—he thought you'd quit. He loved you and didn't want to see you hurt."

"Yeah, well, I showed him." She took a long drink of her lemonade, feeling it puddle in her roiling stomach. She ran a thumb under her lip, wiping the moisture there. "I *passed*."

He looked away, then, and the hard swallow felt like a fist in the middle of her solar plexus. When it was followed by more silence, the depth of it had a colder realization suddenly sinking into her bones. "Jed. I...I passed, right?"

He looked at her. "They gave you a patch, didn't they?"

She slid off the table, stood up, her legs weak, to match her voice. "You didn't answer my question. Jed—I passed the qualifications test, right?"

He drained his bottle. "Listen, it's late. And you're right, there will probably be fire tonight. We might get called out."

"Jed Ransom, you tell me the doggone truth right now. I passed, right?"

His jaw tightened. "No."

She stared at him. Set her bottle down and reached out for the table. "What. Are you. Talking about?"

He made a face, shook his head. "You could have passed. I knew it. But...you fell coming up that last hill during the ninety-minute pack-out test and...well, I knew you had it in you. I knew, by then, that you could do it—you just had the look. And then I don't know what happened. I just clicked the stopwatch. I don't think I realized I'd done it until you got up and passed the finish line. And then I couldn't tell anyone, so..."

"But I finished. *I got up.*"

"And you probably made it. In fact, I'm *sure* you made it. That's why I wrote down a passing time."

"You lied for me."

"But look at you now. One of the best—Kate—"

She walked away from him, shaking her head. "Now, it suddenly all makes sense. I never really got why you were so angry after—" She rounded on him. "No *wonder* you're so hard on the recruits. Because you—you *regret* passing me!"

He gave her a hard look, and she read assent in it, and more. "Oh no. You followed me into the fire that day because you thought you'd made a terrible mistake in passing me and...and because you knew that if I died, Dad would destroy you. You didn't blame me—you blamed yourself."

His jaw tightened. He swallowed, nodded. "I saw you headed right into the fire, and I thought...I've killed her." His breath emerged shaky. "I knew I'd made a terrible mistake, and by then it had gone from bad to worse because..."

"Because I kissed you." She was backing away from him now, her hand over her chest. "That night at Grizzly's, after the test. After they'd handed out our patches."

And from his expression, he was right there with her, caught in the memory. The music low as he pulled her onto the dance floor, ran his hands down her back, molding her to himself as they swayed with a rhythm that belonged only to them.

After years of adoration, of hoping, of proving herself in his world, it had all come together as she'd tucked herself against his sculpted, work-hardened body. She'd curled her arms up around his neck, caught in the aura of the only man she'd ever loved.

She'd pressed her lips to his neck, not thinking, just a crazy moment of abandon. But she'd just landed one of the most elite jobs in the country, felt invincible. Unbreakable.

And in Jed's amazing arms, beautiful.

Then he'd lifted his head and she saw desire in his eyes. When he bent his head to kiss her, she knew.

He loved her, too.

Or at least she'd thought so.

Now, recalled from the memory, her mouth dried. Her voice emerged broken, scratchy. "You regretted kissing me."

"No—I..." He came toward her then, and she batted his hands away.

He looked stung. "Yes, okay. I did. But not at the time. I'd been watching you for five weeks, and every day you became more—I don't know—amazing, maybe. And I thought you'd be okay—I told myself I'd be there, and that I wouldn't let anything happen to you."

His voice softened, his expression almost desperate. "Kate. You were so...happy that night. And I saw you dancing, and I knew the other guys were seeing the same thing."

She frowned. "What are you saying?"

"I just knew that Jock would kill me if anything happened to you—"

Oh, this was just getting worse. "So...you danced with me as a *favor to my dad*?"

"No! Yes. I mean, I—I wanted to be there. I was dying to dance with you. And then, you smelled so good and fit so well in my arms, and I'd sort of been dreaming of kissing you since the day I met you, but you were always off limits and..." His expression turned earnest. "I just stopped thinking, okay?"

"We kissed, Jed. And it wasn't some little peck on the cheek but—well, I don't remember ever being kissed like that. In fact, you danced me right outside and pressed me against the building. And—oh...That's why you stopped. Why you drove me home. Why you practically stiff-armed me the rest of the season."

Until, of course, the Porcupine fire.

Pain edged his eyes.

Jed's voice was soft, apologetic. "I'm sorry I kissed you, Kate." He made another face then shrugged, his voice dropping. "I knew I shouldn't, but I couldn't resist you."

She blinked at him, his words a flame inside her, burning away the romance to the truth. Her voice turned flat. Hard. "So, what you're saying is that I made you, what, lose control of that legendary Jed Ransom composure?"

He gave another shrug and she wanted to lunge at him.

"You...jerk. Here all these years, I thought we had a— well, if not a romance, a moment. That you—I don't know— came after me that day in the fire because you, call it crazy, had feelings for me—"

"I *did* have feelings for you. But I was also your jump partner."

"And babysitter, apparently. Nice job, Jed. Do you kiss all the girls you're supposed to be watching out for?"

A muscle twitched in his jaw.

"So let me get this perfectly straight. Dad sent you to Alaska to make sure I failed. And when I didn't, or rather, when you didn't fail me, which I have yet to figure out—"

"Because you deserved it," he said quietly.

"Isn't that sweet. Except you lied to get me in, which makes no sense whatsoever—and then, after I get my patch, which I *didn't* deserve, you decide that I'm too wanton to be left alone on the dance floor, rescue me by muscling away every other guy—and by the way, I have this suddenly horrifying picture of you threatening every guy on the team should they even harbor a *hint* of interest in me—oh my gosh, you did!" Her mouth opened, and she shook her head, stepped back, her hand up. "Wow. That I didn't see coming—"

"Kate, what did you expect? You were the only girl on a team of sixteen men—"

"Woman. The only woman, who could take care of herself, thank you. And my teammates weren't cavemen."

His dark expression suggested otherwise.

"Perfect. Well, fear not, they kept far away from me the rest of the summer. But let's get back to the point, which is—your superman powers were suddenly weakened by my kryptonite powers of seduction, so you kissed me only to go into a full-out panic over the idea that you'd made a mortal mistake in letting me pass, so you decided to follow me into a wildfire instead of trusting me to get out of trouble on my own. Did I sum that up correctly?"

He swallowed. "You left out the part where you saved my life?"

"Whatever. You wouldn't have been there if it weren't for me. And not just because I couldn't control my chute and get back on course, but for my wanting to be a smokejumper in the first place. And putting you in a position where you had to choose between me and Jock Burns, your hero. No *wonder* you blamed me. Now it all makes *crystal-clear* sense. I can't wait to find out what else you are going to"—she finger quoted—"'protect me from.'"

"Kate—"

"You know, Pete Brooks said that he was in love with me. Maybe you need to head down to the Hotline, see if he's still there. Maybe you can take him out back, work him over a little before he succumbs to my powers."

"Okay, that's enough." He came toward her, and she couldn't help it.

Her hand went up in a slap.

He caught it before it hit his cheek but jerked back, his eyes hard. "What's wrong with you?"

She was shaking even as she ripped her hand from his grip. Didn't apologize. Then, tightly, "I'm not to blame for your broken leg or the fact that you dropped out of smoke-jumping after Alaska. Or even the fact that you kissed me. I will, however, take the blame for calling you a coward. That one's on me."

He flinched then, just slightly.

"What you haven't figured out yet is that you and Dad *both* failed. Epically. Because I'm one of the best smokejump-ers you've ever met—"

"I know."

"No, actually, you don't. But you will. Oh, you will." She

walked past him, off the deck.

When she didn't hear movement, she turned. "I need to get my Jeep."

"Kate, don't leave it like this. C'mon, let's talk—"

"We're *so* done talking. I don't know what I thought— maybe that bringing you up here and talking about Dad, we might find answers or something." She gave a harsh laugh, and it threatened to rip away the fine veil of her control, push out the burn from her eyes. "Boy howdy, did we."

He came off the deck toward her, but she put up her hand. "You said it right, Jed. I promise to stay way, *way* out of your way." She turned and stalked out to the bike. "By the way, you'd better keep your distance. I'd hate for my presence to make you lose control."

Jed watched Kate drive away in her lemon-toned, soft-top Jeep, dread lining his throat as a cloud of dust from the Hotline parking lot rose in her wake.

Somehow he'd made it worse. When he'd told her about Jock sending him up to Alaska, he'd only meant for her to see how much the man loved her. After everything, he thought she needed that.

He hadn't meant to ignite her fury.

You will. Oh, you will.

Words to turn him cold, despite the heat slicking down his back. Kate trying to prove herself could only mean that this might be the summer her luck ran out.

Right before his eyes.

The Hotline still hosted a few late-night revelers, the music spilling out in the gravel drive. He had no desire to go back inside, his instincts confirming her words.

There will be fire tonight.

Indeed, the night had turned deadly, the crackle of lightning occasionally shattering the dark sky over the nearby rumple of mountains.

He gunned his bike and pulled out onto the road, headed back to the ranch house he'd finally purchased just off base.

He couldn't believe she'd nearly slapped him.

I can't wait to find out what else you are going to protect me from.

Maybe herself.

The worst of it was, for the most part, she'd guessed correctly.

The guilt he'd felt when he realized that he just might have ensured her fiery death on a mountain.

He still couldn't explain why he'd passed her that day.

Or, later, why he'd muscled away the likes of her teammates, like Gus or Donut, for his right to dance with her.

But the minute her arms curled around his neck, the minute she leaned her head against his chest, he stopped caring why he'd come to Alaska. He'd lost himself a little when she kissed him, tasting of french fries and the salty tang of her beer, and even that hadn't warned him off or stopped him from kissing her back and surrendering without a thought to tomorrow.

Who knows what might have happened when he dragged her outside of Grizzly's that night if she hadn't whispered Jock's old nickname for him. *I thought you'd never come around, Cubby.*

A jolt of reality. Jock's voice ignited like a blaze in his head. He'd jerked away, disentangled himself, pretty sure he'd left his heart behind in her grasp.

Judging by tonight, he still had the ability to lose a little more of himself every time he got near her. By the end of the summer, he might not have anything left.

She simply didn't get it. *Of course* Jock didn't want her to jump—and it only got worse after their near-death fight on the Porcupine River basin.

Sometimes, in the subsequent years, listening to the stories of her so-called bravery, jumping into fires under conditions that a sane man would run from, Jed went somewhere private and lost it.

Simply sank down, his head between his knees, a hand on a garbage can, a cold sweat shaking through him.

Then he'd drive up to Jock's place to find the man staring glassy-eyed at the stars, going through his own personal trial and execution.

A part of Jed truly believed that deep down inside, Kate had a death wish. And for that, yes, he wanted to reach out and shake her, good.

Or just pull her to himself and never let go.

Probably what he should have done seven years ago instead of shoving her out of his life.

Coward, indeed.

Jed pulled into the gravel drive, parked the bike, and climbed off. The tiny three-bedroom, ranch-style house, a log cabin once upon a time provided by the Forest Service, sat only a half block from the fire base, facing the runway.

If he turned, he could spot Jock's silver Airstream a half mile away on the cliff overlooking the base, watch the lights wink out or blaze into the night, a come-hither beacon.

Not for him.

He pocketed the keys, headed up the driveway. Clearly his roommate, Reuben had returned. With company. Conner's black Ford 150 sat next to Reuben's Silverado.

The absence of Pete's Charger only slightly niggled at him.

"You know, Pete Brooks said that he was in love with me."

He strode up the walk and banged open his door a little harder than he intended.

Stifled a curse.

Reuben and Conner stood in the middle of his living room—his *empty* living room—holding his Wii controllers like golf clubs. A game of Wii Sports-Golf flashed on his new flat screen.

His other furniture, however, hadn't simply been pushed out of the way. Oh no, like a good hand-crew, Conner and Rube had completely emptied the room of anything that could cause trouble, like they might if they were digging a fire line right down to the mineral soil.

"Where is my sofa?" Jed asked just as Reuben took his swing.

"Ah! Crap. It went wide." He turned to Jed. "Really? Don't you know the rules of golf? No talking while someone is taking a shot."

Jed glared at the six-foot-two bull rider. "My end table? My coffee table? My recliner?"

Conner slid off his perch on the dining room table, stepped up for his swing. "We moved them."

"I see that. Where?"

"Pete's room. They're stacked on his bed."

"Stacked..."

Conner lifted a shoulder, along with the hint of a grin.

"His fault for trying to come onto Gilly tonight." He glanced at Reuben who nodded, didn't smile.

Ah. Right. Still...

Jed turned, walked down the hall past Reuben's room to Pete's, the larger one with the king bed. Sure enough—the sofa, recliner, and coffee table lay on the bed, as if exhausted from their labor in the family room. The end table perched on Pete's dresser.

Jed stood there, picturing the ensuing battle between Pete and Reuben. "I'm not amused!"

Nothing.

He returned to the family room where Reuben stepped up for his next shot, his stance wide, holding the controller like a driver.

Jed leaned on the door frame, shook his head. "Tell me again why I agreed to rent you a room?"

Reuben looked up, glanced at Jed, raised an eyebrow. "Quiet on the green."

Jed launched himself at him.

Reuben's shot went off the screen as he threw up a hand to ward off Jed's tackle.

They landed with a thump near the dining room table. Conner moved out of the way, watching.

"Yo! Bro—!" Reuben hooked his leg around Jed's leg as Jed grabbed his arms, yanked them back. "What's your deal?" He wiggled one arm free and jammed his elbow hard into Jed's ribs.

Jed kneed him in the back. "I like my house the way it is!"

Reuben rolled, caught Jed's fist, but missed the other arm grabbing him in a headlock.

Jed felt the man's fists pummeling his ribs and relished it, fueling the adrenaline. He needed this, something to burn off the heat of his fight with Kate.

Reuben head-butted him hard, and Jed's nose bloomed pain. He let go, howling.

Reuben got up, rasping, wiping his face. He bore a scrape on his cheek.

Jed lay there, his eyes watering, just staring up at his two teammates, who peered over at him.

No one said anything.

Then Reuben held out his hand to Jed, who grasped it. As he pulled Jed to his feet, he turned to Conner. "Your shot."

A beat, a glance at Jed, then Conner walked over, reactivated the waiting game.

Jed picked up a chair he'd knocked over from the table and sank into it. Felt his nose. Didn't feel broken. He ran his knuckle under it, just in case, and came away with a trickle of blood. Super. He fished out a bandanna and sat with it pressed against the burn.

Conner's shot landed on the green to cheering from the Wii crowd.

"Wanna play?" Reuben said.

Jed shook his head.

"Wanna hit me again?"

"Maybe."

Conner leaned against the table. "Kate has that effect on people," he said, not looking at Jed.

But Jed looked up at him. "How do you know? You worked out of the Boise base—you two didn't—"

"Chill. Not even close. Kate has a strict no-dating-firefighters policy. But I do remember a few squad bosses who looked like they wanted to drop her out of a plane without a chute."

No dating firefighters, huh? Did that mean she'd dated... others?

And why not? It had been seven years. He shouldn't expect her to pine for him.

Not like he had for her, at least.

Jed checked the blood, found it had already stopped. "If I could, I'd take her wings from her, ground her permanently."

He wasn't sure why he said it, but it came out low, a growl of frustration.

"Seriously? C'mon, Boss, she's awesome." This from Reuben, who'd finally managed par. "I fought a couple fires with her, when she jumped with the Boise team. I've never known anyone who could handle themself in a crisis like Kate. And she has uncanny fire instincts, just like her old man."

"Her old man got half his crew killed. He should have listened to Overhead."

Silence, and Jed closed his eyes. He had deliberately vowed not to talk about this, especially with Conner and Reuben.

Mostly because they still hadn't forgiven themselves for letting Jock run back into the fire. Reuben especially couldn't seem to square himself with it—he heard the guy occasionally wrestling with Jock in his sleep.

"Come again?" Conner said quietly, and Jed knew he might now have a real brawl brewing.

He held up his hands in a gesture of surrender. "It's just that I was there that day. I heard the hotshot super tell them where to go. Jock ignored it."

Reuben put the controller down carefully on the windowsill. Shoved his hands into his pockets, kept his voice schooled. "Jock didn't ignore it. He just knew better."

Jed stared at the men—he knew them, knew they loved Jock. Still, something about their voices... "Okay, what am I missing here?"

Conner shrugged. "I don't know. You read the report. The hotshot team was deployed over the face of Eureka Pass, cutting perpendicular to the fire, getting ready to do a back burn. Jock's team hooked up with the shots, and that's when Jock and Otis had words."

Otis Flannery, former JCHS Superintendent, now working out of Missoula.

Conner continued, his voice even, as if he might be being debriefed. "Otis thought we needed to spread out more, split our teams into three to finish digging out the line for the burn. Jock didn't like it. He said that we'd get cut off from communication and lose our eyes on the fire. Otis was listening to Overhead, though, and he ranked higher than Jock, so Jock fell back to the far end of the line with me, Rube, and Pete. He told Browning, Nutter, Deke, Suds, and Weiner to work the middle and connect the line with the shots higher up the mountain."

"Jim Winner," Reuben corrected. "And Anthony Sutton, both from South Dakota."

Right. Jed knew them all.

Nutter—Doug Turnquist—age thirty, father to a son he never met.

Tom Browning, twenty-four-years-old and son of their small-aircraft mechanic on base.

Deke Johnson, out of Minnesota, age twenty-five, kid brother to a seasoned shot Conner had trained.

Bo Renner, rookie, former running back for the Ember Flames, and town darling.

And, of course, Jock.

Conner folded his hands over his chest, looked away.

Reuben picked up the story then. "We constructed our line, and Jock was ready to start the burn, so we all went to finish hooking the lines together when we heard the shout. The fire was making a run up the middle, coming in fast. They hadn't yet connected the lines above us, so a burnout wasn't possible. Then Otis came over the radio and told us to run toward the safety zone he'd found—up the mountain. But Jock turned to us—and told us to run back, toward the cool black area—already burned over. It was about the size of a football field, and he said if we had to deploy our shelters there, we had enough distance to survive the radial heat. The fire was going to run over us either way, but he calculated the distance to safety and realized level ground would get us there faster."

"Except Otis's route had them going half the distance," Jed said quietly.

"Uphill."

Reuben slid down, his back to the wall. "Jock knew that Nutter and the guys would never make it up the hill. He told them to drop their tools and run to us, but Otis came on the line and ordered them to him."

A heartbeat, then Jed filled in the rest. "Jock ran back into the fire to stop them, try and save them, bring them back down"

"The shots on Otis's crew, the ones working the far edge, ran up the trail," Conner said.

"They had to deploy their shelters," Reuben said. "Four are still suffering from burns, but they lived."

"But the guys caught in the middle—Browning, Nutter, Suds, Deke, Renner, Winner and Jock...well, they simply couldn't outrun it."

"If they'd obeyed Jock instead of Otis, they might have made it."

"And if we'd gone Otis' direction, we would have died, too," Conner said. "But because Jock defied orders, he's the bad guy. Some of the shots claimed that while he was arguing with Otis, the guys could have been fleeing to higher ground, but I'm telling you, Jed, Rube and I hiked that pass, and there was no way to outrun that fire uphill. We lived because Jock followed his gut. And if the guys had listened to Jock, they'd still be alive, too."

Jed closed his eyes, seeing the old man, his dark hair salted with gray under a JCWF gimme cap, staring up at the mountains through his aviators. Always thinking.

"Good decision, bad outcome." Jed glanced at Reuben, then Conner. "His luck finally ran out. It just takes once. I wish Kate would get that."

"Like I said—she has instincts like her old man, Jed. Have a little faith in her." Conner walked over to the Wii, turned it off. The music died. "She certainly has faith in you, dude. According to her, you saved her life a while back."

Reuben stood up, shoved his hands in his pockets. "She told us about the fire and how you hiked out with a broken leg. That's dope, man."

"Yeah, well, she's telling it backwards. I might have saved her—briefly, but it was my fault. I read the fire route wrong, and we had to deploy our shelters. She climbed into mine and held it down for me." He held out his hands, the skin rumpled along his knuckles, still reddened. "I would have died out there if it weren't for her."

Another risk she'd taken to save a life.

"I can't help but think that ever since then, it's like she's trying to punish me for...Oh no."

He ran his hand across his forehead, as if pushing the truth into his head. "That's it. That's *exactly* it."

Reuben frowned at him. "Huh?"

He got up and headed into the dark kitchen, opened the door to the fridge, letting the light and the cool air cascade over him. He grabbed a Diet Coke, closed the fridge.

Conner and Reuben were watching him.

He opened the pop. Took a long drink. "After we'd been rescued, they flew us to the hospital in Fairbanks. I had some pretty bad burns on my hands, and they did surgery on my leg to set it. When I came out of surgery, there she was, sitting on the end of my bed, wearing scrubs. She'd taken a shower, all the soot and grime off of her, and she looked at me with this grin, like, wow, we lived."

More than the grin, however. The tenderness in her eyes, almost an expectation of more of what transpired between them in the shelter and afterwards. The rekindling of everything he'd ignited at Grizzly's. And that's what scared him the most.

"I can admit riding out the fire in the shelter just about took me apart. For the first time, maybe, I realized I wasn't invincible."

And neither was she. Remembering the moment when right before he pushed her to the ground to deploy her shelter, she froze, fear holding her paralyzed, could still waken him in a cold sweat.

"But it did the opposite for Kate. I looked at her in the hospital, and she had this look in her eyes—like someone who's cheated death. We were nearly roasted. I was sitting there with bandages on my hands, my leg in a cast, still reeling from the sound of fire cooking over us, and she was standing there glowing, as if suddenly invincible."

And he'd been too afraid to ask what that glow might be about—the danger ...or him.

He took another drink, and his gaze went to the window. The lights on the deck around the Airstream still blazed.

"I told her to stay away from me. I still can't believe I said that."

But for good reason. Because if he couldn't stop her, then he couldn't watch.

"And stay away she did," he said quietly. "And has been punishing me for it ever since. Taking chances, proving herself..."

Conner glanced at Reuben, back to Jed.

"And it wasn't only about me. She was punishing Jock, too. He'd heard about what happened and came to Alaska to get her. They—we—had a blistering fight. He basically told her to quit jumping, and she pretty much told him where he could put that idea. She jumped with the Alaska team for the rest of the summer. As soon as I could, I headed south, back to Ember. I quit the jump team, started heading up the Shots. And Jock and I had a back row seat watching her jump fires across North America for the last seven years."

The lights over the Airstream finally blinked out.

"And now...lucky me, I've moved to a front row view."

He drained the rest of his Diet Coke then crushed the can, turned and shot it toward the garbage can. Netted it.

"Except, I'm tired of watching. I'm tired of worrying. Kate Burns isn't going to crash and burn on my watch."

"How are you doing to do that? You can't follow her from jump to jump."

"Watch me."

Reuben raised an eyebrow, a smirk on his face. "*Ho*-kay."

Conner, however, drummed his fingers on his leg. "Listen, Jed. We all know she doesn't have to prove she knows what she's doing. She's Jock's daughter—and a trained fire behavior analyst. She wants to be a jump trainer—maybe it's time to give her exactly what she wants."

"What?"

"You're so freaked out about her getting hurt. However, she's never trained anyone, never had anyone she's responsible for. Having someone you care about makes you safer, makes you take fewer risks, right?"

Jed was catching on. "Yeah. If she were to take over the training, the game changes. And maybe then she would discover that you can't have both worlds—you have to keep people safe *or* be their pal. You have to choose."

Maybe then, she would understand why—and deep in her core agree—that expelling her from his life was the only way to save them both.

He waited for them to refute his words, but Conner just nodded.

Reuben made a face. "Well, that sorta hurts my feelings. I thought we were pals. Are you saying you don't care if I die?"

Jed grinned. "Not when you rearrange my furniture."

Jed's cell phone buzzed, and he pulled it off its clip on his belt. "I got a text, I gotta go in. Get some winks, guys. I think we'll be jumping fire by morning."

He clipped the cell phone back on and headed to the bedroom to grab his gear bag. "And put my furniture back!"

Chapter 5

IF HE GAVE HER A CHANCE, they could knock this fire down in a day.

Kate leaned toward the window of the plane and spotted a clear patch of forest, flame lengths of fifteen feet, maybe more, wrapped around black pine and spruce, flickering up as if in morbid greeting.

Not a big fire, yet. Maybe she could let herself breathe. She might even live up to her own overblown, zealous words.

You will. Oh, you will.

Oh, her impulsive, angry, prideful mouth, leading the way yet again right to her doom.

She had no room for fear. Never mind the clench of her gut, the acid crawling up her throat, the way her hands shook. She gripped the straps of her pack, holding on with whitened fists.

She had a legacy to uphold. And now her own stupid declarations.

Three thousand feet below, the two-acre blowup seemed a pinprick amidst the lush ladder fuels of lodgepole, Douglas, and ponderosa pine, climbing along Solomon Canyon up the slopes of the Cabinet Mountains.

The spark had ignited near a campground along the Solomon River, a trickling creek that fed into the larger branch to the south, but narrow enough that, should the winds pick up, the fire could jump the river and head east, toward civilization. Or north, over the ridge, and into a collection of cabins that dotted the hillside.

"It's just a baby!" she yelled above the hum of the plane to Pete who sat next to her, face grid raised, surveying the blaze. Reuben gave her a nod.

She shot a look at Jed, seated next to Cliff O'Dell, their spotter for the run. Jed seemed to be neatly ignoring her as he leaned over a topo map, checked his radio, and talked through fire fuels and scenarios.

The man had appeared wrung out when she arrived at HQ for roll call at six a.m., stirred out of sleep by the siren blaring, echoing up the valley, accompanied by a text on her cell.

Clear Fire—Kootenai National Forest—2 Acres along the Solomon River—Jump 01 responding from Ember.

She didn't even remember getting dressed; already had her gear packed. Jed, Reuben and Pete lived closer—just across the street from the base, and Conner's fifth wheel was parked in permanent residence at a campground next to the base.

The team had barely greeted her when they met in the ready room where Jed outlined the blowup. Then Kate donned her gear—helmet, jumpsuit, parachute harness, supply pack—checked her jump pockets, laced up her boots, and did a quick braid of her hair, tying it back with a bandanna.

Fifteen minutes later, she'd hiked across the tarmac to the plane.

Jed, in his jumpsuit and packs, gave her a cursory once-over, then checked her name off the list and gave her nary another glance as she boarded.

Stay out of my way.

Apparently, he'd taken those words to heart.

She, however, had rolled those words around, feeling the fresh sear of their fight.

Somewhere, deep inside, she must have believed that reconciling with Jed, at least enough to share memories of her dad, would somehow balm the rift they'd never healed.

Instead, she'd managed to turn it from a rift into a canyon. And set herself up for disaster. Yes, she knew how to fight fire, but getting up-close and personal...

Shoot. She tightened her grip on her straps before her entire body started to shake.

No one knew—and she certainly wasn't going to 'fess up that she'd spent the past two fire seasons grounded, fighting fires via computer screens instead of in the field.

"Buddy check." This from Pete, who checked her straps, her gear. She returned the favor. With only five of them jumping they'd all go together, one after another.

Jed first.

She glanced at him, took in his clenched jaw. His first official jump in seven years—she didn't know what was making him break his streak.

Or maybe she did. Maybe he, too, was trying to prove that his fears couldn't hold him down.

Gilly came over the coms, announced their altitude, then Cliff hooked himself into his spotter harness pigtail and opened the door. Cool air rushed in, laced with smoke and the aroma of pine.

She swallowed but couldn't dislodge the burn wedged in her throat. Her pulse thundered in her head, just under the rampant rush of air.

Cliff threw out the drift streamers to gauge the wind currents and find them a safe path to ground. Kate struggled to her feet as the plane banked, hoping to catch a glimpse of the blue, red, and orange drift ribbons.

They fluttered down, the blue one tempted to the flame like a moth. The orange streamer headed south toward a ridge, the third found the meadow, a fifty-foot diameter just east of the fire.

They'd located their landing zone.

Gilly arched them over the ridge, just past the fire, and Kate glimpsed a homestead perched on the side of the mountain. A small corral held horses.

Property. Animals—possibly humans—in harm's way.

They made another pass, and Cliff stuck his head out into the slipstream to assess the drop zone. Then he turned to the jumpers.

"There's about four hundred yards of drift, and the winds are pulling to the west, so stay wide of the fire. The jump spot is in that meadow, just beyond that service road—see it?"

Jed nodded, and Kate willed her heart steady as she worked on her helmet, secured it, then lowered her grid. Jed sat in the door, his feet in the slipstream. The static line to his canopy attached to the plane and would deploy automatically. Although she'd learned to jump on squares—the self-deployed rectangular chutes the Bureau of Land Management used in Alaska—the Forest Service in the lower forty-eight still depended on auto-deployed rounds.

The round parachutes made it safer to land in a forest made up of spears, the kind that could trap a man in a tree.

Cliff patted his shoulder and Jed pushed off.

She couldn't help the urge to lean out, just to make sure—

Reuben clipped his static line to the overhead cable, sat

down, and slipped out next.

When Pete sat down, Kate was still craning her neck. He pushed off just as she spotted Jed's chute, white and fat, a round puff of cloud blooming against the smoky gray sky.

She dropped into a sitting position, her hands on the door, the wind grabbing at her boots. Waited, watching now as Reuben's chute popped open.

Just a baby fire.

Pressure, and she pushed hard against the door and out into the sky.

She didn't have to count, but it came to her anyway. *Jump Thousand.*

Her chute deployed with a quick, hard tug, the quiet soothing the rush of adrenaline as she drifted down to terra firma.

Conner launched himself out behind her—she searched for him and found his chute open by the time she hit *Wait Thousand.*

Grabbing the toggles, she quartered with the wind and aimed for the meadow.

The column of black smoke tried to drag her in, but she steered herself away, into the wind, watching the world become larger, pine trees taking shape, the jump spot looming.

Below, Jed found the sweet spot, hit and rolled, then popped back up to his feet as if he were born to jump.

Maybe, like her, he was.

Reuben, then Pete. She came in soft, playing the wind, and landed perfectly, rolling like a dancer, wishing for a moment she might still be flying as the crackle and snap of the fire prickled her ears. The redolence of smoke drifting from the nearby forest scraped her eyes. They burned, watered.

Finally jumping fire again. This was what she wanted, right?

Jed had already packed his chute and was radioing for the gear drop—chainsaws, the Mack III pump, supplies for a strike camp, should they need to overnight.

She wound up her chute and watched as Conner drifted down, fighting the sudden up-churn of winds, bringing him in just on the edge of the meadow, about fifty yards from the fire.

He landed, rolled, and headed toward them, running from the heat as he wound his chute up.

All five safely down. A good way to start.

Zipping out of her jumpsuit, Kate walked over to Jed. Reuben and Pete caught the crates of supplies attached to chutes, now drifting down from the plane. "I got a good glimpse of the fire as we came in, and I have an idea."

Not a tremor in her voice. All business. Yes, she might survive—even impress.

Jed was studying the topo map, confirming a safe jump with Cliff on coms. Now, he glanced up at her, gave her a quick once-over, as if to make sure she still had all of her moving parts, then sat back on his haunches. "I'm listening."

Really? She'd expected pushback but pounced on this. "The fire is heading northwest, up the canyon, and I think if we can count on the river as a natural firebreak, we can secure the tail with the pumps. I'll stay here and pinch off the flank with a burnout in this meadow and drive the fire north. We can use the Forest Service road as another natural break, reinforce it, and burn out along the edge." She traced her finger along the route in the map that corresponded with the grassy road on the edge of the meadow. "I saw a thick stand of birch near the head of the fire, so if we can drive it there, the low-combustible birch will slow it down. With the leaf litter of the birch duff, combined with the cooler temps and higher night humidity, if the winds decide to cooperate, we'll get this thing to lay down by morning."

"I dunno. If we follow that route, that's forty chains—a half-mile—of fire line dug by five people in sixteen hours," Jed said quietly. "If the winds hold."

"The burnout will work, Jed." Kate kept her voice even, confident while she rolled up her jumpsuit, shoved it into her pack. "Especially if we call in a tanker."

He looked up at her, his jaw set, as if in thought.

It stirred the memory of watching him train, his determination even as a teenager to impress, to become a hotshot firefighter. She'd admired him long before she fallen for him.

Probably, she could admire him again.

"Yes," Jed said. "We'll attack the head with retardant, slow it down, then reinforce it with another load here, along the road." He tapped his finger on the map. "But that means we'll need to reinforce the tail, keep it from turning on us."

Jed glanced past her to where Conner and Reuben had assembled the paracargo—organized the chainsaws, the fuel and tool mixes, flares, and stuffed the personal gear bags with food.

Everything they'd need for an all-day, into-the-night-and-beyond attack.

Jed stood up. "I'm going to scout the head and call in a tanker. Kate, you organize the burnout, Pete, fall in behind her and dig us the fire line."

Really? No argument? "Roger that."

Kate grabbed her Pulaski, pulled her bandanna up over her nose, and surveyed the Forest Service road, a five-foot-wide swatch of dirt and weeds. She chose an anchor point where the road split and headed along the tail of the fire toward the river. Conner and Reuben, carrying the pump and fuel along with hose, had already taken off in a jog for the water source

She watched Jed, already on the com to Overhead, walking straight toward the smoke and ash.

Be careful.

She didn't know where the niggle of worry came from, but she tamped it away.

The more she focused on work, the less she thought about the roar behind her. "Let's do this!"

Pete dragged their gear into the safe zone behind the road. Kate dug in with her Pulaski, leading the way, attacking the earth, and sinking into a quiet, hard rhythm.

She'd never minded the back-breaking work of cutting line. On the bigger teams, with twenty shots working together in crews of five or seven, all digging a line in a rhythm, there was a beauty to it. One man cut away the brush, another ran a saw, clearing out the trees and stumps. Three or four cut into the soil with their Pulaskis, more behind them turned it over with shovels, and a final hotshot with a rake or maybe another shovel left the ground bare.

Between the smoke burning her eyes, the dirt and dust clogging her nose, grinding into her pores, and the sweat from the heat and work saturating her body, working a fire line could crush her bones to dust.

How she'd missed it. Despite the danger of it, the crackle of the fire just behind her, popping and snapping, and the bone-jarring work, she simply loved the camaraderie. Not unlike, perhaps, the brotherhood of battle.

The smoke settled low into the valley. Behind them, the fire gnawed at trees, and in the distance the roar of Reuben's chainsaw lifted, evidence they'd begun attacking the tail as he cut apart smoldering snags and tore apart widow makers.

Pete was breathing hard beside her.

"You and the boss work it out yesterday?" Pete said in between swings.

Kate didn't look at him, unsure how to respond.

"Because I've never seen him bend to an idea not his own quite so fast."

She kept digging, rolling his words through her head. They reached the logging road, and she pulled her radio from her holster. "Burns, Ransom."

Jed's voice crackled over the radio. "Ransom, Burns. You ready to light it up?"

"Affirmative."

"I'm heading down. Keep your pumps out."

The water pumps, five-gallon bladders that they wore like backpacks, could keep a backlit fire behaving, running the right direction. They had nothing against a serious blaze, however.

She took out her lighter in lieu of a drip can. "Don't let it jump the line." As she walked down the cut line, the fire crackled as the grasses lit. Pete walked along, armed with his water can in case anything beyond the line ignited, but they'd scraped out a chunk of earth down to the barest soil.

Footsteps thundered along the path, and Kate looked up to see Jed running down the line. "We've got a drop coming in, ETA seven minutes."

"Just make sure they don't drop it on my fire," Kate said. "Not before it burns all the way to the forest edge."

Jed had the radio to his mouth, communicating with the air tanker.

The meadow flashed over in a sea of flame, the blaze

churning black smoke into the already hazy air. Jed stood a few feet away, his radio to his mouth, looking strong and capable in his green pants and that yellow shirt that clung to his body in a way that outlined everything she remembered about him.

A man unafraid of danger.

Well, most danger.

Then the sky rumbled with the engine sound of a Tanker 38 thundering in from the southeast, the Ember base.

Kate turned, lifted her eyes to the heavens, and spotted the giant Lockheed Hercules 130 with the 3600-gallon fire retardant tank. Still flying high, the retardant pilot was probably making a reconnaissance sweep. The bigger fires used an Air Attack—a smaller plane to guide in the big tankers—but on a blaze this size, the pilot could drop the entire load on the flank without help.

She turned back to the fire.

"Get down!"

She heard the voice a second before she latched onto the source—Jed, flying toward her, his arms spread.

She didn't have time to blink, let alone brace herself before he took her down. He rolled her off the road into the meager protection of the forest as three thousand pounds of slushy retardant rained down from the sky. The 130-mile-an-hour jettison could decimate saplings like matchsticks and rip through tundra down to the permafrost.

Kate screamed and curled into a ball. Jed braced himself over her, tented his arms over their heads, and pressed his lips close to her ear. Deep baritone, solid, calm.

"Close your eyes and don't move."

Jed just knew Kate's luck would run out on his watch.

He layered another splice of oak into the fire, the flames curling around the log like tongues, sparks flickering into the swaddle of night. Cicadas had come to life from the nearby river, hushing over the rocks, silver under the fading moonlight.

He took another sip of coffee, black, too strong, but enough to keep him awake long enough for his team to get some shut-eye and for him to figure out why fate hated him.

He'd given into Kate's plan for the burnout because—so shoot him—he looked at the fire and decided that putting her on the burn line might be the safest possible place.

Instead, he'd put her in the path of a near-deadly slurry drop.

Proving once again that you only had to be unlucky once.

Nice, Jed.

To make matters worse, Kate had barely spoken three words to him all day since his gallant all-out tackle. He'd find bruises tomorrow, and his bones ached from the miscalculated drop from the rookie air-tanker pilot, a mistake that still had him picking mud from his hair and turning his skin red.

And he'd do it all again, without a second thought.

Because for a moment, Kate had turned in his arms, and the wall between them shattered. He'd tucked his head in over hers, rounded his shoulders, and took the onslaught of slurry while she fisted her hands in his shirt, letting him protect her, at least for thirty wet, grimy seconds.

Finally.

Now, caked with mud, soot, dirt, and smoke, he was debating stripping down and wading naked into the river to lather up. Under cover of night, the sky still foggy with the dying fire, he might get away with it.

Especially since Kate curled in a slumbering ball in her sleeping bag in her tent, just on the edge of the assembly. She'd hiked up from the river, the grime washed off her hands and face, grabbed a granola bar and headed to her tent.

After the first botched run, which landed half the retardant inside the line and half out and completely destroyed Kate's plan, they'd had to regroup. With only two rounds of slurry left, Jed had opted to reinforce the tail, direct the fire north, then drop the final load onto the head. As evening settled in, the fire calmed and began to lie down at the birch grove, just as Kate had predicted.

After eighteen hours of fighting, they'd managed to pump water from the river around the entire perimeter, leaving the core to burn itself down to ash.

Jed had finally called it around midnight, and they made camp near the river, past the fire line, in a grove to the south that still stood green. While Pete and Reuben set up the tents, he'd pulled out the fixin's for dinner, boiled water for the MREs, made coffee, finished off a can of fruit cocktail, and finally served re-hydrated beefy macaroni to his exhausted crew.

Reuben wolfed his dinner down, then he and Pete disappeared to the river. They returned twenty minutes later, drenched, hair washed, most of the soot cleansed from their faces, both wearing nothing but their shorts and boots. They toed off their boots and climbed into their tents.

Conner had also disappeared to the river but returned earlier, not quite as clean, fully dressed. He'd hunkered down beside Jed. "You want first watch, or should I?"

The fire could still spot, and Watchout Situation Number 18 said no sleeping near the fire line. In this case, with the fire bedded down for the night and their camp a good two hundred yards from the tail end of the fire, Jed counted it safe enough. Still, "I'll take first watch," he'd said.

Conner had eyed him. "Don't get heroic. You need your sleep too."

Jed had hung a bear pack in case one of the back country animals got ambitious, then hiked back to camp, his mind on Kate.

Something about her silence felt...off.

He probably shouldn't have panicked when Tanker 38 announced the drop. They'd all lived through the accidental dump of a load of slurry.

Pure instinct turned him toward Kate.

What shook him more, however, was the way she'd held onto him. Trembled. Even whimpered as if...

Since the Porcupine River fire, he hadn't known Kate Burns to be afraid of anything. Frankly, that was the problem.

He stilled, his coffee cup halfway to his mouth and cast a look at her tucked in her sleeping bag, her tent flap open, her body illuminated in the glow of the fire. The memory of the afternoon—his body braced over her, muck and slush raining down on him—rushed back.

And Kate curled up beneath him.

He couldn't flush away the expression in her eyes. Fear. White-faced, shocked, overwhelming terror.

He stood up, needing to shake away the sense of it, the deeper memory of having seen that expression before.

We're not going to make it!

His voice, maybe, although he couldn't remember who said it first.

Jed walked over to the silver edge of the river, watching the moonlight run a finger across the boulders, tip the moss with starlight. The lacy wisp of smoke turned the air pungent as it caught in the cooler wind pockets of the night.

Kate, if you don't deploy right now, you're going to die!

He leaned a shoulder against a trio of paper birch, seeing the Porcupine River fire roaring behind her, flaming tongues chewing up trees, thundering, a tornado of fiery destruction.

He had grabbed his own shelter, wrung it out, the agony from his broken leg and the fact that he'd dropped his gloves forgotten in the roust of the wind—

When he'd looked up, he found her just standing there, frozen. White-faced, trembling. "Kate!" He'd grabbed her arm, shook her, and when she didn't respond, he pushed her down, practically tackling her. She came to life then, struggling, thrashing.

He grabbed her helmet. Found her eyes. "Get your shelter on!" Then, because he didn't know what else to do, he tucked his shelter over her, grabbing hers out for himself.

The hairs on his neck singed against the heat, the fire still a hundred yards away, but closing fast. He fought the winds for the shelter, turned to tuck his feet in the pockets in the back, but the shelter unleashed into the hot current. He fell, his leg useless. Worse, he cried out, the pain crippling him.

In that moment, the thought that he would die here, clutching the tundra of an Alaskan forest, fate having finally caught him, seemed secondary to the fact that maybe he'd killed her, too.

And then, there she was. Diving in beside him. Tucking her legs to hold one side of the shelter down. He pinioned his foot into the other corner, pulled the dome over both of them, and she secured her side with her elbows.

He tucked her in under him, her helmet against his, and he wedged his bare hands into the corners, holding the shelter down over the top of them.

"Dig us a hole in the ground to breathe into," he shouted over the rage of the fire.

And then, the heat engulfed them.

Jed leaned up from the tree, gasping, not realizing how he'd been holding his breath. Now he instinctively moved his hands, flexing them against the tight, still-red skin. Sometimes he could feel the flesh searing off against the foil of their shake-and-bake. Could hear his own whimpering in his ears.

Then Kate's voice would return, the whisper of her lips against his cheek. "Breathe, just breathe, Jed." He'd again feel her hand curl up around the back of his neck to force his face down to the cool, damp earth. "We're going to live."

Live. Yes. He threw out the coffee then struggled to the edge of the river, dipped his hand in and washed water over his face. Got on his knees and took both hands now, pulling off his helmet, his bandanna, wetting it and scrubbing away the grime, the black.

The heat.

He wrapped the bandanna around his neck and let the icy water trickle down his spine. Then he sat back on his haunches, lifted his eyes to the sky.

Breathe. Just breathe, Jed.

"You okay, bro?"

He looked up to find Conner behind him, wearing a look of concern.

Jed managed a wry smile. Shook his head, then rewrapped the wet bandanna around his grimy head. "I'm just thankful every time a fire goes our way."

"True, that," Conner said. "Fire's about the most unpredictable thing out there—one minute you think you have it licked, the next you're running for your life."

From across camp, Jed heard a muffled groan, maybe one

of the guys turning in his sleep.

"Not unlike falling in love with a woman," Conner continued. "One minute you think you're headed toward a happy ending, the next you're wondering what you said."

Jed glanced at Conner. The man had his hands in his pockets, staring away from him, as if thinking.

"I didn't know you were dating anyone."

"Not anymore," Conner said, then pursed his lips and shook his head. "It's just that sometimes it doesn't matter what we do. Life—like fire—isn't in our control, and all we can do is show up, armed with our best tools, and take it head on, trust that it'll go the right direction."

For all the time Conner had fought with him on the Jude County crew, Jed had never quite gotten to the bottom of Conner's story. Half computer nerd, half soldier, Conner looked like a surfer in a hockey player's body. Shoulder-length blond hair, parted seventies-style in the middle, with the aura that he could handle himself, Conner had been the one guy who seemingly hadn't fallen apart after the tragedy. He spent most of his off time tinkering on inventions in his trailer. Or playing Wii Golf with Reuben.

Now Conner turned to Jed. "That's what we call faith."

More moaning from across the camp, and Jed identified it as coming from Kate's tent. He hadn't hurt her today, had he? Although after today's workout, no doubt every bone in her body ached.

"I know all about faith, Conner," Jed said quietly. "My dad had faith—or his version of it. He called it gambler's luck and whipped it out every time he decided to bet his weekly pay, our truck, or even our house on some poker game." He met Conner's eyes. "You know what faith got him? His wife dead from pneumonia because he couldn't pay the gas company, buy food, or her medicine. Him, a drunken, grief-filled couple of years that ended up with him robbing a liquor store for about forty bucks. Me and my brother shipped off to live with my uncle while my dad did his stint in Dawson County Correctional."

"That's not the faith I'm talking about. That's faith in yourself—and that kind of faith is always going to let you down. No matter how hard you try, eventually you're going to fail yourself. You can't get it right all the time."

Yes, yes he could.

But Conner apparently wasn't stopping. "And that's the point. We're always going to be overwhelmed, disheartened by our own stupidity, even afraid. Faith, however, says, *don't panic.* God—the One who loves you—has your back. He already knows what you need and wants to provide it."

Jed didn't know exactly how to refute Conner—the words settled on him, hot on his skin. "You sound like Jock, always preaching. But look where faith got him. Listen, I'm not against God, it's just that I've got this. I'll figure it out."

Conner nodded, not really a smile, but no condescension either. "I'm sure you will, bro."

The moaning intensified and, even as Jed turned, lifted into a shriek.

Conner started toward the tent, but Jed grabbed his arm. "I got this."

Because deep in his gut, he knew the source of that scream; had heard it before. He crossed the camp in seconds, then landed on his knees at the edge of her tent.

Kate shook in her sleeping bag, crying out. "No!"

For a second, he couldn't move.

He had no idea that—well, that she hadn't really escaped the flames that day, either.

Then he climbed into the tent, found her arms, and

pulled her up to himself. "Kate! Shh—it's me. It's Jed. It's just a dream—"

She drew in a long breath, recoiling. Her eyes opened, fixing on him. Not really, however, seeing him. Then her mouth opened, as if in another scream. Short of letting her wake up the entire camp, he didn't know what else to do.

So he kissed her. Just wrapped his hand around her neck and brought his mouth down on hers, hard. The shock of it had her stiffening in his arms.

"Shh," he said against her lips, then kissed her again.

His first kiss was hard, a reflex more than tenderness.

The second contained emotion, a spur of need, or desperation.

What started as a reflex slowly morphed into a release of everything churning inside him for the past week when she showed up beautiful and frustrating and the flesh-and-bone realization of everything he couldn't dare hope for.

A needy, thirsty, devouring kiss.

She still hadn't exactly kissed him back, despite her mouth softening to receive his, but she seemed to relax, her hands reaching up to curl around his arms, as if holding on.

Then, slowly, the desperation turned to something deeper.

Better. He softened his kiss, moving his hands to cradle her face, his thumbs caressing her cheeks.

He trembled, the smell of her—smoky, sweet—enveloping him. She let out a sigh, and he became aware—too aware—of every inch of her as she slid her arms around his waist and pulled him closer.

Oh—he could nearly taste his heart in his throat, the urge to step too far over the line, the heat of desire quickening inside him.

He put his hands on her shoulders, intending to draw back when, suddenly, she tightened her grip on him and started kissing him back.

It began with the softest, sweet sound of surrender in the back of her throat, then emerged in something urgent, alive, her mouth opening to him, an offering that just about unraveled him when he tasted her tongue, the coffee on it, and behind it, her own latent yearnings.

And everything he'd banked since dragging her out of Grizzly's those many years ago fanned to flame.

Kate.

He wrapped his arms around her, feeling the soft skin at the waist of her shirt, aware somewhere in the back of his brain of a sound, the warnings blaring. The sleeping bag had fallen to her waist, she wore just a T-shirt, and it raked to life the inferno growing inside him. The kind that, if he didn't take a breath, would make him press her back into the soft folds of the sleeping bag, stretch out alongside her, and finally dive into all the feelings he'd been running from for seven torturous years.

Her hands had smoothed against his back, lighting a fire under her touch.

I'm trusting her to you, Jed.

And shoot, apparently the spirit of Jock still hovered between them.

"Stop." He pulled away from her, breathing hard, swallowing, his heart lodged in his ribs. "Please—"

He took a breath, raised his head.

Awake now, she met his gaze, her own eyes wide, her hair disheveled, her lips moist, half open, as if in shock.

They breathed together, just staring.

"You started it," she said quietly.

"You were...crying out in your sleep."

She raised an eyebrow at him. "Was I?"

He nodded, possibly too briskly, his heartbeat still betraying him. "So I—"

"Kissed me."

"Woke you up."

"Oh." She ran her tongue over her lips, as if remembering. "Is this how you wake up Pete or Rube when they're dreaming?"

He gave her a look. "Yeah. Especially when they're having a nightmare." He scooted himself back, still trembling, and noticed that she let him, folding her arms over her chest. "Sorry. You were screaming, or starting to, and I didn't know what else to do."

And wow, that sounded lame, but he couldn't—*wouldn't* let her know just how much she undid him, left his world spinning.

He was, frankly, still trying to catch his breath.

At his words, her mouth pinched, and she gave a short, quick nod. Then she looked away, wiped her cheek. As if she might be...crying?

And now he was a jerk.

"I'm sorry, Kate. Let me get you a drink."

"Don't baby me!" Her eyes flashed. "Get out—"

"No—okay, yeah, I will but—Kate, listen. Maybe—were you dreaming about the, you know...the fire? I mean, do you want to talk about it?"

"I don't." Her face hardened. "I'm fine. Just...tired."

"We all are."

That stopped her. She ran her gaze over him, from his wet bandanna to his grimy, whiskered face, to the sodden clothes.

Her voice dipped and she sighed, the anger flushing from her voice. "I never thanked you...for today."

He blinked at her, not expecting—

"But it was unnecessary, Jed. I was fine."

Of course she was. "It was three thousand pounds of slurry—you would have been knocked flat, maybe seriously hurt."

"I *was* knocked flat," she said, and raised an eyebrow, her mouth tweaking up.

In that moment he glimpsed the girl he'd known before, the one who didn't have her dukes up quite so far.

Then she vanished. "But out here, I'm just one of the guys. You can't protect me—"

"Watch me!"

He didn't mean to shout. He pursed his lips, looked away, fighting his breath. "I have to, Kate...especially now," he said finally, revealing too much. He should just get up and crawl out the door.

Silence. He dared a glance at her. He expected ire, or maybe just contempt.

But she wore such sadness, it engulfed him, swept away words.

"Jed, you're not responsible for me anymore. Dad is gone."

Crazy, unfair heat burned his throat. "I know that." Except with Kate in his arms, it seemed that Jock had shown up, given what Jed had had on his mind.

"But this isn't really about Jock." And then, because he didn't know what else to say but the truth, "It has to do with the fact that I can't take the idea of you getting hurt." Shoot, but he was already there, saying the words he vowed to keep to himself. "I can't watch you die."

She frowned. Bit her lip. Sighed. "Jed. Every time you tackle me or try and protect me, you take your eyes off your job. And when you take your eyes off your job, you miss something. And then someone else—not me—gets hurt. And *I* don't want that."

He knew that too well, because that was exactly his reasoning for not wanting her around. At least on the fire line.

"So, if we're going to work together, you have to consider me one of the guys."

His gaze raked down her, deliberately taking in her curves under that milky white T-shirt. "I don't think there is a guy alive, here or anywhere, who could do that."

Her mouth tightened in a pinched bud of something—frustration, maybe. She reached over and pulled on her grimy yellow shirt. "Better?"

No. "Yes."

She fumbled for something in the dark and came up with her water bottle. Uncapped it and drank. Then, wiping a knuckle across the moisture on her upper lip, "Did I ever tell you about the summer my mother left us?"

He watched her cap the bottle. "No. You just told me she left when you were twelve."

"For another man. A small, quiet man who didn't fight fire. He lived in Ember for two years, which included two summers when my dad was out on the fire line. I'll never forget the day she told Dad she was leaving—she simply came home and packed our bags. Mine and hers. We were living in town then, in one of the fire cabins, and she had me halfway out to the car, me kicking and screaming, when Dad pulled up in his pickup, fresh off the line. He was black from head to foot, his eyes bloodshot, his voice raspy with smoke, and told her that she could leave, but she wasn't taking me. She told him that this was no life for a little girl."

Jed could almost picture Kate, knobby knees, wiry thin, her red hair in braids, in cutoffs and a T-shirt, tears streaming down her face.

"They made me choose. Dad stood there, telling her that she could take me during the summer, yeah, but that he wanted me the rest of the year, and Mom said something to the effect of *over my dead body*—she didn't want me growing up around fire. She said there was too much danger, death—and the last thing she wanted was for me to turn out like him. She said she couldn't love a man who loved fire more than her."

She was running her finger around the rim of the bottle, and he so longed to push the hair back from her face, to see her beautiful eyes.

"And my dad just stood there and looked at me and I knew... I was already like him. Not only did I spend every summer riding my bike down to the fire camp, helping him pack food bags and listening to him talk fire behavior, but there was something about the life of a firefighter that I longed for. I couldn't leave. So...I chose my dad."

And that revelation nearly took him out. Because even as she looked up at him, her mouth tipping in the saddest of grins, he wanted to reach out and pull her to himself.

To wrap her in his arms and tell her how sorry he was that she'd never gotten to say good-bye.

"You meant the world to him, Kate," he said gently. "You should know that every summer he tracked you down everywhere you went. When the teams would come in from a booster callout to join the Boise or McCall team, or when he flew down to Missoula, he always quizzed them about you."

She looked up at that, nodded. "I did the same thing. Once we were on the same fire in Idaho, and I thought...I'll just go up to him and say hi. Just like that. Maybe he'd look at me and see that I was safe, that I could do this job, that he—and you—had trained me well. But when I went to look for him, I found out he'd flown out the morning I arrived."

She put the bottle down. "That summer Mom left he moved us to the camper. I think it was so the people at camp could keep an eye on me even when he wasn't there. And I spent every waking minute at fire camp, cooking, helping organize the equipment, running errands, looking over the shoulders of guys like Otis and Big Jim Renner as they plotted fire attacks. I learned fire, and the minute I turned eighteen, I joined a crew."

"I remember. Jock couldn't stop you, since he didn't run the Shots, but he didn't take that well."

"About as well as you did." Again, the smile, sweet, and it took no imagination at all for him to understand why he'd let her pass jump school. Or that he would again.

Shoot, she got in his head, tangled his brains.

"These guys are my brothers, my family. You understand that, I know you do."

He nodded.

"You're my brother, too, Jed."

She touched his arm, traced her fingers down to his hand, the flesh still rippled there. He held his breath at the way her touch could light him up.

Maybe it had the same effect on her, because she took a breath, lowered her voice, moved her hand away. "Okay, perhaps we were a bit more than that. Or wanted to be."

He could just reach out, grab her hand back—

"But not anymore. Let me do my job. You do yours. We'll survive this summer and maybe even become friends."

Friends. The word should be a balm, something soothing, but it only reached into his chest, made a fist. "Yeah," he said, his voice only a little strangled.

"Which means you have to stop tackling me."

"Kate—"

"And *especially* sneaking into my tent and kissing me."

His mouth closed, tightened into a grim line.

She gave a soft, rueful laugh. "Don't worry. It'll be our secret. Because I'm terribly aware that you weren't the only one doing the kissing."

And was it his imagination, but did she look away, as if embarrassed?

"But I'm going to blame that on stress, and not a little fatigue, and the fact that you've always been an excellent kisser. And, please, let's just forget it happened."

Oh. Well—but she lay down, rolled over, her back to him, pulling her sleeping bag back up. "We have work to do tomorrow. Get some shut-eye."

He hesitated, probably too long, because she added softly, "Not here, Boss."

It was the "boss" that sent him sheepishly out of her tent, zipping it up behind him.

CHAPTER 6

KATE BLAMED JED THAT the nightmare had found her. If he hadn't tackled her, hadn't held her in his arms, the demons would have stayed safely locked away.

She stirred the last of the coals of the campfire, now swimming with river water, the charred wood soggy and impotent. The dawn rippled pink just above the horizon, bleeding into the pewter gray of the night.

Behind her, the guys packed up the last of the tents, the sleeping bags, their gear. Nearby, Jed stalked through their camp, the radio to his mouth, calling in their status.

The redolence of ash, smoke, and the dying cinders of the fire haunted the air, but a febrile peace had settled upon the charred, whitened forest, resetting the forests back to seedling. An occasional burn did a forest good—especially one littered with logging slash, dark and seedless. A cluttered forest rotted, grew up, and ached for a cleansing fire, a restart.

Exactly like she'd had with Jed, last night. She couldn't believe she'd awakened, thrashing, sweating, crying, out of the dream of being cooked alive to the rush of being locked in Jed's arms. She'd clung to him, desperate, losing herself in something greater, the longing that still flamed inside.

Almost as if the dream had continued, turning from

nightmare into her wildest, forbidden fantasy.

"Conner, radio in when you get to the head, tell me what you see." Jed, over the radio, on his way into the day. She glanced at him in his grimy clothes, a layer of whiskers on his chin, looking dangerously heroic, devastatingly competent.

The urge to trust him stirred inside her.

Almost absently she touched her lips, tasting his mouth on hers, feeling his hand around her neck, the urgency as he kissed her, his touch molten.

So she'd kissed him back, forgetting herself, the fire line, and even the fact that she'd vowed to never—ever—kiss Jed Ransom again.

His skin had been cool and fresh, his hair wet, and she'd wrapped her hands around those amazing arms, holding on.

Until, of course, he came to his senses. And she reluctantly took a grip on hers.

She'd stared at him in the flicker of firelight, fighting to still her racing heart, hating how she longed to reach for him again. Safe. Solid. Strong.

What she'd so needed two years ago, when everything turned to ash in her life.

She knew, when he'd tackled her, protecting her, that the smart, independent Kate should push him away. But the Kate that still apparently lurked inside had reached out, surrendering to the memory of just how amazing it felt to be in the arms of Jed Ransom.

That scared her most of all. Because in her nightmares, she'd returned—not to the Porcupine River fire but to the one that had truly sidelined her, turned her into a mess of frayed nerves, stolen her wings, and grounded her.

And the minute Jed stepped into her tent and woke her up, catching her in his arms, the shaking, the roiling in her gut, the sense that at any minute she might come unglued—it all vanished.

Jed Ransom, once again, holding her together. Which meant that no matter how far she ran, how many times she jumped, how long she tried to deny it, she still needed him.

He was bending down, packing his bag now, his strong, wide shoulders pulling at his shirt. *Do you want to talk about it?*

His words lodged in her heart, rooting around all night.

It. *Their* fire.

The two hours of hell, huddled together, holding down the fire shelter. Him trembling with the pain of his hands, finally surrendering to whimpers and then gritted screams as the blaze scorched his skin.

Her, reaching for the edges of the shelter to relieve him, his skin peeling off against the searing fabric of the tent.

She'd hadn't yet escaped the dichotomy of being roasted alive set against the calming presence of Jed's embrace, his moist breath on her neck, his low voice telling her to hold on, that they would live.

Across the campsite, Jed clipped his walkie onto his belt and pulled his gloves over those wrinkled hands. When he looked over at her, she glanced away.

They'd never talked about what happened next. How, after the fire had passed, turned to crackling and embers around them, she felt his skin turn cold, his breathing hiccupping, suddenly erratic.

"Conner has already walked the perimeter of the fire, says there's no spotting, so we'll start mop-up. Then I'm going to see if I can pinpoint the source and confirm what sparked this."

She would never forget his whitened expression as he slid

into a full-out delusional panic. Nor how he'd ripped himself free of the Kevlar cocoon, angry, afraid, leaping up into the blackened moonscape of the Porcupine forest.

Shock—she'd recognized it from their EMT training and knew that the fire could still kill him. The memory of him shaky on his feet, his eyes wild, could still send a tremor of cold panic through her.

"Kate?"

She looked up at him.

Jed was holding the map open and now frowned at her. "You okay?"

She nodded, but her gaze fell to his hands, hearing now his voice, his groan of horror as he'd looked at them, moaning as he'd dropped to his knees, his face crumpling.

She distinctly remembered her heart stopping at his gut-wrenching cry. Then his blood pressure dropped, and he'd faded away into blessed unconsciousness.

"I'm just...I just—yeah. I'd like to see where the fire started, too." She picked up her helmet, her Pulaski, her pack, and headed toward the fire line, the memories grinding up to press moisture into her burning eyes.

Kate, don't leave me. I need you.

The last thing she wanted was him knowing that somehow, despite herself...she'd never gotten over him.

"Let's separate into sectors, we'll get this thing mopped up faster." Jed motioned to his crew, indicating on the map where they should begin work.

Conner headed out with Kate along the tail, through the burn area, toward the center. While he felled snags and cut apart burning stumps with his chainsaw, she used her Pulaski to turn over piles of white ash and rake through coals. Then she applied water from her pump and scattered the fuels.

The buzz of saws hummed in the air, the work dirty. Her eyes teared, and her nose was thick with snot, her mouth sawdust dry as the sun burned down on her neck.

She and Conner finally made it to the river, and she used her bandanna to cool her neck as she sat on a rock and took a long swig of now-tepid water.

"You do the work of two men, Kate," Conner said, wiping his face.

"Thanks."

"Nice to be back in the fight?" He uncapped his water bottle.

She glanced at him. "I guess, yeah." She lifted a shoulder, watching him as he ran his shirtsleeve against the moisture on his forehead.

"I have to admit, I was surprised to see you show up in Ember. I mean, after the Buttercup Rim fire I thought I'd never see you again."

She froze then, studying him, but he seemed to not have a clue that he'd unseated her. "What?"

He pulled out a granola bar, offered her a bite. She shook her head.

"I was on the mop-up crew. We heard all about the blowup, how you got trapped. Pretty tough stuff."

She fought to keep her voice easy, her breathing metered. "Yep."

"They said you were in the shelter for nearly two hours."

She nodded. "It wasn't that hot, just long burning. And in the low area I got trapped in, I thought maybe the air would be toxic."

No one had to know that, actually, she had followed exactly in Jed's footsteps and gone into shock.

And he hadn't been there to keep her warm, calm, or hike her out to help. Oh no, she'd unraveled completely on her own, nearly incoherent when her team finally found her and airlifted her out.

Now, she leaned over, filled her water bottle in the river, and didn't look at Conner, keeping her voice even, cool. "I hadn't realized the word got out."

"It didn't, really. I was just there. And the Buttercup range is notorious. I think they've had like two hundred and thirty entrapments in the last ten years. That's a lot."

"It was my fault. I was separated from the crew, on lookout, and waited too long to evacuate." *God isn't a parachute, and someday you're going to find yourself in over your head.*

Her dad's prophecy finally came true as the flames licked the edges of her shelter.

She shook her hand to free the tremor, capped the bottle, then tightened it, and clipped it to her belt. "It's no big deal." She stood up, wondering if the question lingered on her face. Did Jed know? Had he discovered she'd spent the past two years in counseling, working the desk at the National Fire Agency in Boise, wrestling her fear into submission?

Suddenly his protectiveness made perfect sense.

What a joke—she was a legendary, hotshot smokejumper deathly afraid of fire.

She tied her wet bandanna around her neck. "Ready to get at it?"

But Conner wasn't moving. He stared out, away from her, up the river. "I'm pretty impressed that you went through another fire alone—and came out unscathed."

She gave a wry chuckle, lifted a shoulder as if his words weren't lethal.

But he stood up, met her eyes. "Or *did* you come out

unscathed, Kate?"

Her mouth opened. "I—"

"It *is* a big deal," he said softly.

She swallowed, studied his face, and uttered her worst fears. "Does Jed know?"

Conner's mouth tightened into a grim line, at least a little compassion in his expression. "I don't know. He hasn't said anything. Probably not—I didn't see him until later that summer when I joined up with him for a Minnesota fire."

"Please—don't tell him. I'm fine." Now. And she would be, if everyone just left her alone, let her do her job.

But Conner searched her eyes, as if unsure. "Just because you're afraid doesn't mean you're weak, Kate. It makes you more aware of what you can lose, how fast—"

"I'm not afraid. And I don't need you—or Jed—worrying about me." She said this with a sharper edge than she intended, but he didn't flinch.

"Right. Ho-*kay*." He picked up his chainsaw. "And just because someone cares about you—even tries to protect you—doesn't mean they don't respect you."

She frowned at him. "I don't need anyone to protect me either."

He shook his head. "You know, for someone who's spent her life working on a team, you know nothing about what it really means."

He shouldered the saw, headed along the shore toward the black.

Oh, yes, actually she did. Every costly, brutal, betraying nuance of it.

She followed Conner into the dying smolder.

The mop-up work burned away the rest of the day, the

sun dying in a rose-gold fiery sigh beyond the Cabinet Range.

Jed caught up to them as they were hiking back to camp. "There's a truck coming to fetch us at the campground. Conner, take the gear and meet up with him. Kate, c'mere—I want to show you something."

Jed looked as if he'd spent the day sloshing around in ash and mud—his face flecked with dirt, smudged into his two-day beard, his hair sooty, his yellow shirt smeared, stained, and dirty beyond repair. But he hiked through the forest, energy radiating off him. "I followed the burn pattern, all the way back to the campground, and I want your opinion on something."

He did? She trudged through the ash behind him, her boots sifting up white powder as she stepped over charred trees and scorched rocks.

"We thought, at first, that fire was started by a lightning strike. But when I got to the site this morning and saw how the fire had spread, I realized that it started here, in this campsite. Which is strange, because the area was cleared out by fishermen, free of large pines, or anything else that might act as a conductor. When I got here, I couldn't find a tree or any other charred remains. So I started hunting around."

They stood in a makeshift fishing campground twenty feet from the river's edge. Kate made out a warped cooler, a blackened tent. "I certainly hope whoever was fishing got away."

"Yeah, well, I radioed in, and no one has heard a thing about a camper, so we might actually have a fatality," he said, walking to the campfire ring. "The fire was called in by some homesteaders who saw the smoke. I was already in the office, monitoring the lightning strikes, and by the time of dispatch the fire was probably already an acre."

He kicked a can, blackened and charred, into the fire

pit. "Let's hope whoever camped here was long gone." He crouched near the fire ring. "I thought the fire might have started here, from a stray spark. The valley is so dry right now it wouldn't take much to light the entire thing. But looking at the V-shaped pattern, the fire started not here, but over there." He pointed to an area just a few feet away where concentrated ash from a blaze which, according to the pattern indicated, had ignited a fallen oak and the brush around it.

Kate bent down, feeling through the blackness. "Look." She pulled out a melted plastic cylinder about thirty inches long. Warped, with what looked like wings, gnarled on each side. "Is it a flare?"

He took it in his gloved hand. "No. It's a drone—like a weather drone." He turned it over, rubbing the surface. "Conner's been working on something like this to help us fight fires."

"Maybe it crashed. Does it carry enough fuel to ignite the forest?"

"Some do—depends on the drone. I'll take it back with us."

She got up, dusted off her hands. "Report it to Overhead. They'll send some investigators out, take pictures, poke around."

He dropped the drone into his pack.

She shouldered the Pulaski, turned to head back to the campsite.

"Kate, I wanted to ask you something."

Oh.

She didn't know why his words sent a cool finger down her spine. What if he had simply been waiting to get her alone to tell her he knew about her past? Maybe he'd been watching to see her reaction to fire—and yesterday's panic after the slurry drop, coupled with the ensuing nightmare, only made him realize she was a hazard on the fire line.

He couldn't work with someone who couldn't be trusted not to come apart at the first hint of flashover.

She turned, wary—

"I need your help."

"Huh?"

He stood, his Pulaski over his shoulder, met her questioning look with one of his own.

"You saw what happened at the Hotline Saloon. I'm losing recruits—and morale. I've been thinking about it all day, watching you work. No one knows this job better than you. What would you say if I asked you to help me train the rookies?"

She stood, nonplussed, just blinking.

"Listen, I get it. And I can admit that I don't...well, that I don't approve of the way you take too many risks. But you're fire smart, Kate, and you're an expert jumper, and..." He shifted, brought the Pulaski down, dug at the dirt. "As much as I hate to admit it, the cubbies could benefit from hanging out with you."

Despite his cool tone, the way he kept his distance, offering the job almost offhandedly, she had a feeling what it cost him to say that.

But work with Jed every day? After last night's kiss? Yes, it settled there right at the top of her mind, especially when he stepped up to her, smelling of smoke and fire and danger and looking so painfully handsome despite the sweat that trickled down from his temple into his rough thatch of whiskers. No, this could be a bad, very bad idea.

Talk about getting burned—her fragile, still-healing heart couldn't take another go-around with frustrating, let-me-save-you Jed Ransom.

Maybe he saw her hesitate—more out of shock than apprehension—but he must have thought he needed more oomph to his request because he stepped closer, lowered his voice. "Isn't that what you want? To train the best, just like your father?"

He knew how to find her tender flesh, push a thumb into it.

She nodded. And apparently she had no control over herself when Jed stood this close, lowered that deep baritone, because she added, "Is that what *you* want?"

She didn't know what kind of answer she expected, dreadfully aware of the one she suddenly, desperately wanted.

In her wildest dreams, they fought fire side by side and heated up the nights in each other's arms for as long as they both should live.

And how crazy was that—because she'd always told herself she wasn't the marrying kind. The kind to stay home and settled down. Like father, like daughter, right?

She looked away, lest he see the imprint of her hopes in her eyes.

Apparently he hadn't. Jed picked up his Pulaski, stepped away. "I want to save lives and fight fire. In that order."

She took a breath. "Right," she said. "Me too."

"Good." His expression warmed. "Like you said, we're going to need all the jumpers we can pass. And, apparently, I'm begging you to stay."

And this was exactly how she'd gotten-in trouble before, falling for his easy smile, the smoky, sweet texture of his eyes.

Oh, she shouldn't do this again. Except her voice, her brain, had decided to jump first, to leave her heart hanging. "Yeah. I'll be glad to help."

"Perfect. Bright and early tomorrow morning then." He whirled around as if to stride away, and she nearly bumped into him when he stopped, turned back. Took a breath. "And please, Kate. Don't make me regret this. I'm counting on you not to do anything stupid."

The warm feeling dissolved into a puddle of black. Her mouth tightened, but she gave him a hard, crisp nod. "Don't worry, Jed. I promise I won't get anyone hurt."

His mouth tightened as she stalked past him, the embers of their barely rekindled friendship neatly snuffed out.

Somehow, with his suggestion Kate train the recruits, Jed had awakened the ghost of Jock Burns.

Jed couldn't help but feel he'd traveled back in time to his days as a recruit, drenched in sweat, wrung out, yet mesmerized by a leader who just didn't know when to quit. And who made the entire thing seem like some sort of intense Outward-bound vacation.

Kate had clearly adopted Jock Burn's magic recipe for team success—hard work plus prepared fire fighters, mixed in with generous amounts of camaraderie.

Oh, goody, goody, a three-mile run, but Kate had cold water and time off waiting for them after today's PT.

The recruits were actually grinning.

Jed stood on the running board of his truck, holding the stopwatch. Overhead, the blue dome of the sky stretched cloudless, not a hint of rain, the air crackling with heat across the compound. The sun glared on the tarmac, bright off the red-and-white hull of Gilly's Twin Otter jump plane, and the Air Tankers sat parked in orderly rows, gassed up and ready for a callout. The buzzing of an air compressor from the dome metal hangar suggested repairs or maintenance checks on one of their ancient Russian An-2s.

Kate had changed out of her Forest Service uniform into a pair of black running pants, an athletic shirt, her hair braided into two red pigtails and held back with a teal bandanna. She now stood at the head of the assembly of the remaining recruits. Apparently, she planned on leading the pack while Jed remained behind to harass the stragglers.

Figured.

It would help if she didn't look like she belonged on the cover of *Fitness* magazine, her curves outlined in that purple V-backed running shirt.

She climbed onto the back of his truck, and he averted his eyes from her legs.

"Today's run is just practice—you won't get cut if you can't finish the three miles in less than twenty-two minutes and thirty seconds. But if you can't pass this run next week, you'll be cut, game over. Got it?"

She glanced down at him, and he knew she added the last for his sake—he'd already had it out with her once for coddling the team.

Give them a chance to prove themselves, she'd said yesterday afternoon as they watched the recruits practice their landing rolls. *I didn't get it the first time either.*

Yeah, well, look where letting her prove herself had landed him. Replaying their nearly combustible kiss in his head into the wee hours of the night, evoking even more memories all the way back to Alaska, and wishing he'd had the sense back then to send her packing back to Montana.

Then, maybe he would have gotten her out of his system, and she would have moved onto something safe, like grizzly taming, and he would be training the team with some grumpy, hard-bitten, bald and paunchy smokejumper from Missoula.

The sun hovered above the horizon, still cruel as the recruits lined up for their run, Kate in the middle. The base seemed hollow today, the standby barracks ghostly with the sight of so many pickups, motorcycles, and motley cars baking away in the parking lot.

Someone was unloading a truck of dry goods into the supply warehouse, now depleted of food and gear. A few more cars parked in front of the head shed where dispatchers, weather heads, and division commanders monitored the progress of the Glacier Rim fire.

The Jude County hotshot team—with Conner, Reuben, and Pete attached—worked mop-up on a fire in the nearby Glacier National Park, helmed by a smokejumping team out of Missoula.

"Go!" Jed started the watch, and the runners left him in a poof of dust and grunts. He hunkered down into his truck, put it into gear, and let it roll behind them.

In three weeks, Jed just might have a team ready to add to the attack, thanks to Kate and her morale-boosting encouragement, her stories of jumping fire, and not a little dare and challenge she threw out, especially to the youngsters—CJ, Tucker, and Ned.

Not to mention Hannah Butcher. The minute he'd introduced Kate as their jump trainer, Hannah glued to her like she might a big sister, seeing perhaps a kindred spirit. Kate's addition to the training team lit a new fire under the recruit, and Hannah gritted her teeth as she bumbled landing after landing, refusing to give up long after the two other female recruits had walked off the course.

More, the young recruit bore adoration along with the fire in her eyes when Kate got up to teach. Like today, during

Kate's class on letdowns staged in the training area of the base. Located in an acre or more of meadow set off by a chain-link fence, the training area housed the jump tower and receiving berm, the letdown practice platform, the landing roll simulator, an old Twin-Otter, decommissioned and grounded, and the obstacle course, worn and muddied.

Hannah had stared at Kate, hanging twenty feet up in the letdown simulator, as if mesmerized.

Yeah, well, him too. Kate turned into an acrobat when she donned jump gear.

"The first thing you have to keep in your head is that if you're coming into the trees and you don't spot an opening, steer toward the smaller ones. And don't try and grab anything—that's a great way to break an arm," Kate had said, dangling in her gear as if she'd just landed in a giant ponderosa.

Jed had stood at the edge of the crowd, sweat trickling down his back, hoping she wouldn't bring up his brilliant tree landing from so many years ago. Just thinking about it made his leg ache.

"Once you're hung up, you want to check your chute and see how secure you're hung. You don't want to tie off to a chute that will break free halfway down."

And there it was, the quick glance in his direction. He wanted to raise his hand and suggest that he'd snapped his leg *before* his stellar letdown that crashed him fifty feet through the branches back to earth. But, well, he couldn't be sure. Everything after he'd plowed into the black spruce turned fuzzy until he woke up, Kate untangling him from his rigging.

"Also check for loose lines around your neck. You don't want to strangle yourself the minute you cut yourself free. Once you're sure you're free, go ahead and rid yourself of your reserve, then grab up your letdown rope. Take about six feet—leave the rest in your pants pocket. You don't want to drop it."

She had her rope out, demonstrating how to wrap the rope through the D rings, then slowly lowered herself to the ground, landing with a soft crunch on the grass.

Showoff. But, okay, not a bit of daredevil in that move, and everyone, with her patient instruction, landed their letdown. Especially Hannah, who might have been a climber in an earlier life.

It could be that Kate had a soft spot for Hannah, too, because while Hannah seemed fearless in the air and while dangling above the ground, she couldn't seem to nail her PLFs—parachute landing falls. Kate spent an hour during lunch instructing Hannah on her landing rolls in the sawdust pit.

Now, Hannah seemed determined to prove herself as they ran. The runners had passed the first mile marker, Kate now out in the lead with Tucker Newman, the snowboarder from Minnesota. Jed had trained him three years ago, when he'd shown up to join the shots, and had a fondness for the quiet, hard-working kid. He bore high hopes Tucker would make it onto the team.

Kate set a brutal pace—less than eight minutes a mile, in blazing heat, but next week would be with full gear—boots, uniforms—so perhaps this was mercy. Even in Alaska she'd always nailed the workouts, her red hair a beacon for the recruits who hadn't spent off-season in training.

He probably should forgive himself for passing her, his guilt misplaced. After all, she seemed exactly the person she claimed to be...the best smokejumper he'd ever seen.

At mile two, he drove past the stragglers, shouting out times, then headed up to the front and to the finish line marked by the base entrance. There he climbed out and leaned against his truck.

Kate rounded the corner ten feet behind the leaders—Tucker, and then CJ, the rodeo junkie from eastern Montana.

They surged by him, racing at the end, and Jed clocked the pair in well under twenty-one minutes. Kate flew in at twenty-one minutes, point three seconds.

She stood at the finish line, her hands on her hips, catching her breath as he called out the times.

Her gaze, however, hung on the stragglers—the two preppies out of Chicago, a former linebacker from nearby Kalispell, and Hannah.

Hannah pushed hard, wheezing, her short legs fighting to get her time.

Jed showed Kate the time as Hannah crossed the line, ahead of the final three stragglers.

"She'll make it," Kate said and walked away.

"Hey, Boss!" CJ came running up to him, sweat pouring off his temples, down his yellow T-shirt. With a thicker upper body than Tucker, muscles used to swinging a rope and wrestling a steer, he probably had to work twice as hard as Tucker for the same run time. However, with their different backgrounds, the two combined for a lethal pair. "A bunch of us are heading over to Hannah's place for some BBQ ribs her dad's been smokin' all day. Kate said to make sure I invited you."

Kate said?

Jed glanced at her retreating form now in a light jog toward the jumper standby shack. They'd barely spoken other than conversations about training, and he had only himself to blame.

He could still hear his stupid words ringing in his ears. *Please, Kate. Don't make me regret this. I'm counting on you not to do anything stupid.*

Way to win friends. Any goodwill he'd cultivated by inviting her into the training he'd eviscerated with that comment. Evidenced by her follow-up. *Don't worry, Jed. I promise I won't get anyone hurt.*

He'd wounded her, he knew it, but maybe being the bad guy would remind her that she had a responsibility. In a week she had to make the hard choice to send hopefuls like Hannah packing. Making friends with the recruits would only make the final cut more brutal.

"I don't think so, CJ. But thanks for asking."

CJ lifted a shoulder. "Kate said you'd say that, too."

She did, huh?

CJ jogged off, leaving Jed sitting in his truck, stewing.

Which was why, two hours later, Jed found himself showered and sitting outside the mountain home of Hannah Butcher's parents, owners of the local grocery store. The Butcher's lived on a ridge overlooking the town in a ranch-style log home with a hanging basket of red geraniums by the green-painted front door and a chainsaw-carved bear holding a welcome sign on the porch.

Jed parked his bike, listening to the music—a Brad Paisley song—spilling out of the backyard, the scent of hickory chips and sweet barbeque turning his stomach in a roil of hunger. Laughter lifted, and he could swear he heard Kate's— sweet, high, a giggle that belied her tough-as-nails exterior.

Maybe this was—no, *for sure* this was—a bad idea.

Despite the gnaw of hunger teased by the fragrance of dinner, he didn't belong here. He wasn't one of the team, and he shouldn't forget that.

He climbed back on his bike.

"Jed!"

Kate, of course. He looked up and saw her coming around the end of the house, holding a glass of lemonade, looking cute in a pair of jean cutoff shorts, a green T-shirt that did unforgiveable things to her eyes. She wore her hair in a high ponytail that made her look about sixteen—an age and look he remembered too well.

"I thought I heard your bike. You're not leaving, are you?"

He lifted a shoulder, and she gave him a look of exasperation.

"I know Conner and the guys aren't back yet. So what are you going to do? Go home, put in a cardboard pizza, and play Wii?" She ran her finger around the top of her cup, looked away. "Listen. I know we haven't talked, really, since we got back, but I appreciate you pulling me onto the crew. And I think we have a chance of graduating most of them, right?"

"You're doing a great job."

She smiled at this, a light in her eyes, and shoot, but if it didn't brighten his own darkness. He should give her a compliment more often.

"Come around back. Get to know the recruits. They worship you—"

"I think we should keep it that way."

She laughed, and it could slay him. "I know you want them to believe you walk on water, but being a little human can't hurt you."

"I could say the same for you," he said. "They think you're invincible."

Her smile faltered then, and he frowned, a little unnerved. Of course she thought of herself as invincible, right? Wasn't that what—

"Yeah, well, everyone's invincible after they've had a taste of Hannah's father's baby back ribs. Ray uses this special rub, smokes them for five hours." She licked her lips, an action that got his attention. Then she hooked her arm around his. "C'mon. Just a plate of food, and I promise, you don't have to talk to anyone. You can just perch yourself in the corner, eat a plate of ribs, and glower." She winked. "You know, be your usual self."

He gave her a sardonic look but reluctantly gave in and followed her around back.

CJ and Ned sat at one end of the table, their hands gripped, arm wrestling, while Tucker hung out near the speakers, flirting with a couple of girls Jed didn't recognize. "Smokejumper groupies," Kate said softly. "Tucker is a hot item."

No doubt. Along with the preppie boys from Chicago, one slow dancing with Marissa, who'd washed out earlier in the week but had stuck around, it seemed, for other reasons. Another group of jumpers hung out by the smoker, talking with Hannah's dad.

Ray had logged years as a hotshot before settling down to open Butcher's Grocery. He now wore oven mitts and an apron as he pulled a tray of ribs from the smoker and brought them over to the picnic table. One of his helpers slid them onto a cutting board and began to separate the ribs with a knife.

Kate tugged Jed's arm, and he headed over to the action, picking up a paper plate on the way. Homemade baked beans with crunchy bacon, potato salad, pickles, biscuits—he loaded up his plate.

"Jed Ransom—I didn't realize you were training this bunch." Ray dished him up a pile of ribs. He wore a baseball cap over his thinning hair, the hint of white in his sideburns, his expression warm. "I thought you'd be out with the hotshot team."

"A new gig this year. Taking over for Jock."

As soon as he said it, he saw the man breathe in, swallow hard. Then he glanced at Hannah. Jed followed his view.

She stood holding a baby on her hip, wearing a clean, yellow training shirt and jeans, her blonde hair braided down the nape of her neck. The baby played with her necklace as Hannah talked with her mother, an older version of herself, right down to the blonde hair.

With a start, Jed recognized the baby. "That's Nutter's baby?"

"My grandson," Ray said, his smile dimming. "Gemma isn't having a good week—we took little Buck for the day—probably the entire weekend."

Gemma Turnquist, wife of Doug, aka Nutter, one of the hotshots who'd never made it out of Eureka Canyon.

"Doug and she tried for four years to have Bucky." Grief edged his eyes. "Poor man never met his son."

And Jed had lost his appetite. He set the plate down, but Ray reached over and picked it back up. "We all died that day, Jed. But we can't stay dead forever. We're trying here, and Hannah..." He glanced again at his young, capable, strong daughter. "She's been dreaming of being a smokejumper ever since Jock came and talked to her fifth-grade class. I could kill him, but it hardly came as a surprise. After all, that's where I met her mom—on the fire line back in '63. So what am I going to do? Lay down and forbid her to jump?"

Jed had no words. Ray handed him back the plate. "Just train her well, Jed. And if she passes, then I'll leave the rest up to God. And her jump boss." He glanced at Kate. "She's the spittin' image of her old man, isn't she?"

Kate stepped onto the dance floor with a group of rookies, doing a line dance he didn't recognize. She was grinning, clapping, spinning, her long tan legs moving with the beat. Leading the pack as naturally as if she'd been born the alpha.

"Yeah," Jed said, his appetite returning. He met Ray's glance. "I'll take care of her," he said, meaning Hannah. Or, rather, all of them.

He settled on a folding chair, balancing his food on his knees as he watched Kate dance, laugh, her eyes shining. CJ came over with a glass of lemonade and mercifully made no comment about Jed's sudden appearance. Hannah's mom passed him a homemade chocolate chip cookie, and he added that to his plate, feeling satiated as the night slipped in around them, the wind rustling the poplar and fir, stirring up the piney scent of the backyard retreat.

He could almost forget the fact that in a week half of these recruits might be packing up for home, others donning gear and jumping into the deadliest fires in America.

And with one sharp turn of luck...

No. He was here to make sure luck didn't have anything to do with it.

Someone turned the music off, and, to his surprise, he spotted Ned—Reuben's cousin from Minnesota, with his curly, short dark hair, brown eyes, rangy, tall frame—sitting down with a guitar on his knee. He plucked out a mournful tune, then to the encouragement of the audience, lifted his voice in a song penned by some Irish band about Montana smokejumpers. Jed had heard it before and found himself humming along.

A hand on his shoulder startled him, and he looked up to find Kate. "You should play your harmonica," she said quietly. "They'd like that."

"I didn't—"

She reached into her back pocket and pulled out his

Hohner, still sheathed in its black case.

"It was in your bike storage compartment. I saw it there when I stole your helmet the other day."

Oh. He made a face, shook his head, but as Ned finished his song, she stepped forward, and his stomach clenched.

C'mon, Kate. Don't make a fool out of me.

"You all probably don't know that our boss, Jed, plays a mean harmonica. More than once he's serenaded us to sleep in a strike camp."

Serenaded her, maybe, because he couldn't remember playing, much, for the ears of others after he'd left Alaska.

"Play us a song, Jed," she said, turning and holding out the harmonica. He felt the dare in her words, however, lightly spoken.

Shoot, she could make him do things— "Fine." He got up, swiped the harmonica from her grip, and was rewarded with her victorious smile.

He warmed up with a quick version of "Oh! Susanna," embellishing with a warble, the sound twangy in the night.

A few of the recruits hummed along, a couple sang.

Kate leaned back against the table, her cup up to her mouth as if to hide her grin.

"What do you want to hear?" he said when he finished, his gaze on her.

"How about 'On Top of Old Smoky?'" CJ said, and the crowd laughed.

He fitted the harmonica back into place and drew out the song, letting the notes hang in the air like the scent of the hickory, tangy and sweet.

One of Tucker's fan girls leaned against him, and Tucker draped his arm around her, pulled her close. A couple of the rookies slid down to lean against the house, singing along.

Kate slid onto the table, swinging her legs, humming.

Friendly eyes on him, instead of wary. Eyes that might see past his dark scrutiny to a man who had been in their shoes, who thought about more than just fire. Smiles that suggested respect, if not the adoration they gave Kate.

"One more," Kate said as he finished. "How about my favorite?"

Her favorite. Oh. A few eyes turned to her, as if curious about the intimacy of the request. *Oh, Kate, you had to bring that up.*

But the world, for a second, seemed to dim, and then it was only her and him and a song.

He brought the harmonica to his lips again, and the words she'd sung hung in his head as he played the notes, long and languorous, the hymn twining out to turn the crowd solemn.

Great is Thy faithfulness, O God my Father...

Jock's favorite song, really. Something that went along with that faith on the fire line that Conner talked about. Jock had sung it so many times his crews knew it by heart.

A few in the audience had started humming along, turning somber as if drawing in the words. Ray picked up the lyrics, started singing in a resonant tenor. "Morning by morning new mercies I see..."

Kate was smiling, her eyes shiny, nodding her head to the beat. Jed's breath clogged as if it were in his chest.

He re-sheathed the harmonica to rousing applause and got up, waving it away. "Should you cubbies pass next week, you might hear me play again. Maybe." He couldn't look at Kate as he walked back to his chair, his heart thumping.

She had a mean streak to make him pull that song from the past, and now that the last tones had died, the words settled inside him, turned into a burr. He pocketed the harmonica, picked up his lemonade to drain it.

"Thanks—"

He heard Kate beside him and glanced at her. Swallowed. Shrugged. "I gotta get going."

A crease appeared between her eyebrows, then it cleared, and she stepped back. "Yeah, right. I get it."

No, actually, she didn't, but he couldn't go there. Not without doing something stupid and pulling her away from prying eyes, demanding from her exactly why she'd had to rouse the memory of him waking up in her arms, still cold with shock, the night arching above them. And her singing. Softly. Enough for him to lean into it, yearn for it. To want to believe.

All I have needed Thy hand hath provided—

A song that could still make him marvel at the fact they'd lived, right through until morning, that maybe God had sent a team in to find them, and that yes...He provided.

Except, maybe she did get it, because she turned back to him, her voice low. "You weren't the only one out there who lost faith that day, Jed. I was hoping maybe we had a second chance to find our way back."

He had a retort, but she caught his gaze, letting him see a softness in her eyes.

We'll survive this summer and maybe even become friends.

So that's what she wanted. To repair the broken places inside. The only difference was, "I never had any faith to begin with."

Her smile dimmed, and he felt like a jerk. But she'd started it, making him, ever so slightly wonder, even hope, that he could have two worlds—love and duty.

He sloughed her hand from his arm. "Hang out with

these cubbies all you want, but don't think for a second you can really be their friend. This is a tough job, and they have to be a little afraid of you to listen to you on the line. Never forget, it's up to you to keep them alive."

Her smile vanished. He threw his plate in the trash, finished off his lemonade, and waved to Ray. "Be ready to make cuts starting on Monday."

CHAPTER 7

Jed just couldn't be right. Kate wouldn't let him.

Hang out with these cubbies all you want, but don't think for a second you can really be their friend.

Except, the longer she worked with Hannah on her landings, the more she watched her roll awkwardly off to hit her shoulder or be dragged away by her chute, the more Jed's words turned into claws, sank in, and burned.

Kate should have cut her three days ago instead of letting the agony continue until today, Hannah's last qualifying jump. She jumped like a pro, her positioning perfect, reacting in the tower to every kind of mishap.

She simply couldn't land.

Hooked into the pigtail that secured her to the plane, Kate kneeled down, her head in the slipstream, watching the jump streamer. The wind took it about three hundred fifty feet, drifting to the east.

"Take us to jump altitude, Gilly," she said through the coms and felt the plane bank and turn, climbing from fifteen hundred feet to three thousand. She turned to Ned, who would be jumping first, and raised her voice above the roar of the air. "Hook up!"

Ned wobbled toward the front of the plane, holding onto

his reserve to keep it from deploying accidentally. Fully loaded with sixty pounds of gear—chute pack, reserve, dangling
front pack of personal gear, and letdown rope in his pants
pockets—he weighed close to two hundred fifty pounds.
Suited up, with the harness strapped tight, Ned could barely
stand up, let alone walk. He clipped his static release line to
the overhead cable, and crouched next to her. Behind him,
the eleven recruits who still survived lined up, fighting for
their footing.

"I've got three thousand," Gilly said in her ear.

"Get in the door."

Ned sat on the edge, his feet in the slipstream. She pointed out the drop zone—easily seen by the orange flags. She
could barely make out what she suspected was a very stressed
Jed Ransom armed with a clipboard and a video camera.

Sweat trickled down her back. *Please, let them get this
right.*

She tapped Ned's shoulder, and he launched himself out
of the plane. The static cord flapped, tensed, then fluttered
back as his chute deployed. She checked—no tangles, and
he'd grabbed his toggles.

"Next!"

CJ clipped in, sat down, and seconds later, vanished.
Again, the chute deployed. Two down, ten to go.

She worked up the line—Tucker, then one of the Chicago boys who'd miraculously made it this far, then one of
the other female recruits, and on down the line. Each one
clipping in, sitting in the door, a tap, and they disappeared.

Hannah stepped up last. She clipped on her line, gave
Kate a thumbs up. "Remember to roll!" Kate said, but her
words were unnecessary. No one understood the stakes better
than Hannah.

She tapped her shoulder, and Hannah flung herself out.

The line fluttered, tensed, snapped free, and the chute popped out, filled hard. Hannah soared upward.

Kate leaned back, gave Gilly the all-clear to land. Gilly banked, and for a second, Kate rolled back into the belly of the plane. She grabbed at her line to catch herself.

"Sorry!" Gilly said.

Kate righted herself then rolled over to survey the landings, when, out of the corner of her eye, she spotted the malfunction. Apparently Hannah's chute *hadn't* fully deployed, a suspension line twisted around one side, causing the canopy to flatten.

Hannah began falling again at terminal velocity.

Kate lay flat on deck, screaming into the wind. "Cut away! Pull your reserve!" But Hannah was wrestling with the line, tugging to free the knot.

Kate slammed her hand on the floor of the plane, her breathing hard. "Cut away!"

But now Hannah was spinning, both toggles loose, her vision probably blurring.

In a second, she'd be completely disoriented and unable to pull her reserve.

Kate didn't have a parachute. But she was doing the math—if she dove now, she might be able to catch her, although falling at ninety miles an hour meant a very small window of success. Still, maybe it could work—she could grab onto Hannah, cut the chute away, pull the reserve—

Angry tears washed her eyes as her breaths tumbled out, one over another— "Cut! Away! Cut—!"

Then, suddenly the knot broke free. With a snap, the canopy filled, and in a second, Hannah's plummet arrested and she floated, soft, quiet, ethereal. She found her toggles and began steering into the wind, toward the drop site.

Kate rolled onto her back, breathing hard, her heart in her ribs. Stupid, angry tears streamed down her cheeks—panic tears, really, because she felt nothing but the adrenaline drain.

Stupid girl. Why hadn't she cut away? In a spin like that, the force could cause disorientation, delay reaction times. Maybe she hadn't been able to get her hands on her cutaway cord.

Kate pressed her hands to her chest, willing herself not to hyperventilate. Whatever the case, she needed to get on the ground, now, and throttle the girl.

By the grace of—well, God—Hannah hadn't simply arrowed into the ground, leaving another training casualty on the psyche of the base and community.

Kate sat up and strapped in as Gilly landed the DC-3, then piled out, running across the tarmac. Hannah had already landed, was conferring with Jed, going through her landing, her grid up, her chute wrapped over her arm.

She looked up at Kate, beaming. "I landed it! Or—nearly, landed it. Jed's giving me a satisfactory on the PLF—"

"Are you kidding me? You nearly *died*. Did you not think to cut away? Why? *Why?*" She could feel herself unraveling, but she couldn't seem to pull back. "Hannah, you have to keep your head. React faster than that—"

Her voice fell, turned hard, still shaking. Jumpers were eyeing her, turning away. "You nearly bought it today. You should have cut away and pulled your reserve at the first sign of a malfunction. You took a terrible risk trying to untangle—you don't have time for that. If you can't learn to make split-second—and safe—decisions, then smokejumping is no place for you."

Hannah had gone white, her breath coming in long and deep, her expression tight. She stared at Kate, then back at Jed, who looked at Kate with raised eyebrows.

"What—?"

"That *was* her reserve chute," he said. "The first ripped right after deployment."

"What?"

"Yeah," Hannah said. "I looked up to check and saw it flapping. So I cut the chute and deployed the reserve. But it got tangled. I knew I had no other choice but to fight the knot out, so I just kept working with it."

Even as she fell. Keeping her head in the game.

Kate bent over, grabbing her knees, breathing hard. "Okay...okay."

Jed's hand touched her shoulder. "Kate, just calm down, she's fine—"

She stood up, rounding on him. "Are you serious? Just *calm down*? And what would you have said to Ray Butcher if his daughter had done a swan dive out of the plane? Calm down?"

Except, Jed *was* calm. Standing there with his clipboard, his mouth a grim line, evaluating Hannah's jump, her landing. "It's over, and there's nothing you could have done about it anyway. You just have to trust that you've trained her well."

Kate stared at him, raking through her reaction on the plane, the way she'd nearly—yes, seriously contemplated—leaping out without a chute after the recruit.

He frowned, then, as if he could see it, the churning of possibilities in her mind. "Kate—you weren't thinking—"

"I need a minute." She straightened up, glanced at Hannah. "Good job."

But she didn't feel her kudos. What she wanted to do was rip the chute off Hannah, march her to her car, and drive the kid home. Except, no, not kid—woman. Full grown, twenty-one-year-old woman who'd spent three years as a hotshot, worked her backside off, and who deserved the chance to jump.

Kate climbed into her Jeep, bracing herself on her steering wheel, leaning forward to just breathe, hold herself together.

And then it settled into her bones. No *wonder* Jed had freaked out when he'd seen her break away her main chute, fly after Pete.

Or even before, when he'd followed her off course so many years ago.

She reached out, her hands shaking, and started her Jeep.

Jed had gathered the recruits, probably giving them final instructions about tomorrow, when he'd let them know if they'd passed their final test.

She'd let him make the decisions. She couldn't bear trying to decide who lived—or didn't.

Putting the Jeep into gear, she turned around and took the back road through the base, up the hill to the Airstream.

The generator hummed as she pulled up, which meant the AC would be on and the water pump working. She banged inside, shut the door, pulled off her sweaty jump clothes, and climbed into the shower.

Bracing her hands on the small cubicle, she let her legs give way, slid down into a crouch, and cried.

Just excess stress, at first, but then it became something else. Tears for the men who'd watched friends fall from the sky and others who sat on Eureka Ridge and heard the screams of their dying comrades over the radio in the canyon below. She cried for Conner and Pete and Reuben and the scars they carried and for the families who couldn't sleep, fighting their overactive imaginations and grieving the loved ones who would never walk through the door.

She leaned her head back under the spray and cried for Jock Burns, for the man she'd known and the one she didn't, for the hero and the legend. And finally for the daddy who had loomed larger than life when he donned his smokejumping gear, then came home and told her stories while they traced the stars.

Wow, she missed him. With a burn, right through the marrow of her chest. She pressed her hands there, moaning, and cried for their last good-bye, the one in Alaska, when he'd asked her to stop jumping, please.

She'd walked out of his life without a backward look.

She cried for herself, for the stranglehold death had on her regrets, her vacant tomorrows, and the fact that she finally understood.

Please, Kitty, don't jump fire. It will consume you, if you aren't careful. And it's not if you get hurt—it's when. God isn't a parachute, and someday you're going to find yourself in over your head.

She could wail at her retort, still branded in her brain.

I don't need God—I have my own reserve.

Yeah, she'd proved that, hadn't she? Knew exactly how it felt to be on her own in the middle of a fire.

She pressed her hands to her face. *I'm sorry. I'm so sorry, Dad.*

She finally lifted her face to the spray as the undulating emotions shook out of her, turning her hollow, breakable.

And, so keenly aware of exactly why Jed had pushed her away.

No one wanted to watch someone they care about—even

a friend—die.

She stood up, lathered her hair, washed, then turned off the water and stepped out of the shower, wrapping a towel around her.

Movement at the front of the Airstream, through the windows, caught her attention. She slipped into her bedroom, peering behind the door

Jed. On her deck, holding a clipboard, pacing.

What—? She dried off her hair, not bothering to comb it, then got dressed, pulling on a T-shirt and a pair of loose jeans. Padding out barefoot, she closed the door behind her, carrying a couple bottles of lemonade.

He'd changed clothes, and by the look of it, showered also. His hair curled in dark, dampened ringlets around his temples. He'd pulled on a heather-gray T-shirt that outlined his still-wet body and a pair of black cargo shorts, wore his signature off-duty flip-flops. "We need to talk."

She handed him a bottle of lemonade then slid onto the bench, her back to the table. "I don't care what you do, Jed. Pass them or not." She shook her head. "I can't be responsible for what happens."

He raised an eyebrow. "Seriously? Um, that's *exactly* what you are. You trained them, and we're doing this together. You and me. Figuring out if they get what they worked so hard for or go home, destroyed."

"Nice, Jed. Thank you for that." She shook her head. "I hate this."

He opened the lemonade, took a drink, then set it on the table. "Yeah, well, guess what. Only two didn't pass with flying colors. Our Chicago boy and—"

"Hannah."

"Yep."

He sat down next to her—and oh, he smelled good. Not just soap, but a rich, woodsy cologne, all topped off with that Jed Ransom aura of power. As if nothing ever ruffled him.

Except it had, it did. At least once.

She looked at him. "But that's not what you want to talk about, is it?"

One side of his mouth tugged up, his eyes growing soft. He shook his head.

"Jed—I...can't. I've put it behind me, and you should too."

"Our...fire... is actually not what I was referring to either."

Huh?

"I wanted to talk to you about this." He handed her a piece of paper from his clipboard. She took it, her chest tightening as she read the e-mail from her former boss in Boise to Jed. "Why is your boss—or ex-boss—asking me how you're doing?"

She swallowed, trying to find her voice. Nothing.

"He said he read about the fire in an agency report and said he didn't know you were back on the fire line. What does he mean...*back on the fire line?*"

Oh. She handed the e-mail back to Jed, who got up now, standing in front of her. She scrubbed her hands down her face. Sighed. "I was trapped a couple of years ago, over in Idaho, on a fire."

He just stood there.

"I was alone, and..." She shook her head. Looked into the horizon where the sun hovered, as if waiting, too, for her explanation. "It was a low-burning fire, but I was caught uphill, and—it was everything you taught me to look out for, and I was stupid."

"You deployed your shelter," he said quietly.

"I was in for two hours. The fire wasn't that hot—just wouldn't die down."

"Were you hurt?"

Hurt. She tightened her jaw, shook her head.

Silence, and she finally glanced up at him. She couldn't unravel the look on his face, in his beautiful smoky blue eyes, part concern, part confusion, and it moved her to an answer. "I had...a rough time afterwards."

More stupid tears, but she knuckled them away. "I was pretty scared, and I..." She couldn't look at him. "Shoot, Jed. Why does it matter? I'm fine now, and I don't want to talk about it."

"Another thing we're not going to talk about?" He slammed the clipboard down on the table next to her. "I'm sorry, Kate, but yes, we *are* going to talk about this. Because apparently something happened and if it's going to affect the team—"

She launched to her feet. "It's not going to affect the team. I'm fine. And I will be fine forevermore. I'm not going to take any risks, and I'm not going to get anyone hurt."

Hurt, or maybe anger flickered in his eyes. "What *happened*?" he asked, his voice so low it rumbled under her skin, unseating her.

Kate stood there, staring up at him, his eyes now so dark she hadn't a clue what he might be thinking. "Fine. I...I had a nervous breakdown. A full-out meltdown. They had to hospitalize me."

She got a reaction then. His eyes widened, his mouth opened. Closed. He swallowed. "Oh, Kate—"

She held up her hands, backed away. "This is why I didn't say anything. I didn't want you to think that I was—"

"Broken? Scared? Alone? Sheesh—" He tunneled a hand through his hair—it stood on end. "You should have called me—*why didn't you call me*?"

"Why didn't I...are you kidding me? I couldn't call you— you're the last person I wanted to know how I'd failed."

"Failed? How you *failed*? You didn't *fail*, Kate. You lived through another terrifying entrapment, and the thought of you going through that alone—" He turned away, breathing hard now. She thought she heard a muffled curse word. Then another, this time more creative. He turned back to her, his face just a little whitened. "I should have been there for you. I should have been the *first* person you called. No one understands better than me—I'm so sorry, Kate."

She simply blinked at him, nonplussed. "You're sorry?"

"Of course I'm sorry! I've been sorry every single day since I told you to stay away from me in Alaska. I figured it out about two point three seconds after you took off that I was an idiot, and if I hadn't been strapped to my bed with IVs hanging off me, my hands bandaged, my leg in a cast, I would have chased you down the hall and all the way to Boise, begging your forgiveness. Or wanted to—if I wasn't such a prideful jerk. I know you didn't deserve any of what I gave you, but I was so..." He clenched his jaw, shaking his head, and in his eyes ranged the same clutter she'd seen before— frustration, pain, horror, fear—and something else. Maybe something stronger, worth waiting around for.

"I was so scared," he said finally, quietly, looking away. "I didn't want you to leave, but I knew that if you stuck around, if I *let* you stick around, then I'd keep making stupid decisions trying to protect you."

"I don't need protecting—"

He held up his hand. "I get that. I know that, but it's in my blood, Kate. I can't *not* protect you. I can't not look at you every time you jump and hope—and pray hard, I guess—that your chute opens. And if it doesn't, that your reserve shows up. And that you don't get impaled by a tree, and that once we're on the ground you don't get hit by a snag or some falling rock or, God forbid, chased by a wall of fire. I dream about it—more often than I'd like to admit—you standing there, frozen, the fire roaring up behind us, your beautiful eyes filled with terror. And I wake up shaking, in a cold sweat. My greatest fear is that you'll freeze again."

"No. I heard your voice in my head. *Deploy your shelter.* You were there, Jed. At least in the beginning."

His Adam's apple moved in his throat. He blew out another breath as he walked to the edge of the deck. Held onto the rail.

She watched his rumpled skin turn white against the railing.

Oh, Jed. She walked up, put her hand on his back. He drew in a quick breath as if her touch wounded him.

"I didn't tell you, either, because I didn't want to scare you."

"I'm already scared, pretty much all the time, Kate." He looked down at her. "Every time you go up I feel a little sick." He sighed. "But I know that's the way it is. I can't keep you from jumping—well, I can..."

She dropped her hand, frowned.

"But I won't. Not anymore. Because I think...I *hope* you finally get it." He turned to her, took her hands. "You were a little crazy today with Hannah." His thumbs moved over her hands, sending tingles, heat up her arms.

"She nearly died, Jed. Of course I freaked out. She's my protégé. And maybe like a kid sister to me and—"

"And you care about her."

"A lot."

"Exactly." He stepped closer to her, touched her cheek. "Except you're not in love with Hannah."

Then he bent down and ever so softly kissed her. Sweetly, lingering, not even testing, but as if he'd been waiting, banking the fire to a slow burn until this perfect, singular moment.

He tasted of the sweet lemonade, still cool on his lips, and she didn't quite know how to react, except—

Yes.

She'd been dying to kiss this man—*really* kiss him—since that day seven years ago at Grizzly's when she'd taken him in her arms. The panicked kiss in the tent didn't count, wrought from adrenaline, filled with regret.

This kiss she meant.

She'd never stopped loving Jed Ransom, from the day he appeared on her doorstep all the way to the night after they'd nearly perished in their fire shelter, when she'd held him again, this time trembling in her arms.

Jed. She pressed her hands to his amazing, muscled chest. He made the slightest moan, deep in the back of his throat, moving his hands around her, pulling her in close. Then he angled his head to deepen the kiss, nudging her mouth open, diving in as if kissing her might be the way he stopped time and delivered them both into a pocket of reality where fire and loss and fear couldn't find them. Where, for a delicious, blessed moment, they clung to each other, safe.

They'd had it once, briefly, and he brought them to it again with the smell, the sense of him, strong, capable. *We're going to live through this, Kate.*

The past seven years fell away, puddled around her as she sank into him, wrapping her arms around his neck, losing herself in the breadth and height of surrender.

He backed her up, and she felt the table against the back of her legs. Then, his hands were on her waist and he lifted her to sit on the table. She leaned back, and he caught her chin in his hand, lifted her gaze to his.

His smoky blue eyes glistened as his eyes roamed her face, his expression so tender it lodged her heart in her throat. He caught her wet hair, twining it between his strong fingers before he nestled it behind her ear, trailing his hand down her neck, back to cradle her face. "Oh boy, am I in trouble."

She frowned but added a smile. "Why?"

"I can feel Jock staring down at me, and I'm just bracing myself for the lightning."

She looked up, over his shoulder. "Sky looks clear."

"Yeah, but he's in my head, screaming."

She laughed. "Yeah, well, Dad was always a little overprotective."

Jed's expression turned solemn. "I promise to not hurt you again, Kate."

"You can't promise that," she said, smoothing her hands down his sculpted chest. Wow, she remembered this too, being pressed against his body as he shielded her from the heat of the fire.

His thumb drew down in a caress. "Then I'll try. I won't freak out every time you jump out of a plane, and I'll do my best to trust you." He touched his forehead to hers. "And if I can help it, you'll never have to go through a fire alone again." She reached up, touched her fingers to his dark whiskers. "That'll probably take a little faith on your part."

He drew in a breath. "A little." Then he leaned down and kissed her again.

Jed didn't need a parachute to fly.

He sat at his desk, amidst the weather reports, requisitions for food, supplies, and equipment, and a briefing from the new hotshot crew boss, Axel Calhoun, and fire couldn't touch him.

His brain zeroed in on one thing—the fact that Kate sat in the loft, repairing parachutes. He had a vision of himself sneaking in, wrapping her up in one of the silken clouds, disappearing with her in his arms.

He wasn't sure how he'd gone from standing at the edge of her world to an all-out dive into what he'd been quietly longing for his entire life, but he wasn't going to look up, see a possible tear in his canopy.

Jed leaned back in his desk chair, balancing it on two legs as he peered out into the main area where Weather and Dispatch monitored lightning strikes and callouts from other stations. The squawk box buzzed out updates now and again, but nothing to make him worry.

That'll probably take a little faith on your part.

Kate's words. And, while he'd shrugged them away before, now they found him, burrowed in, sat there, itching.

Maybe not. Because something had shifted in Kate when she watched Hannah plummet from the sky—a realization, finally, of exactly how it felt to watch someone you've trained die—or nearly—on your watch.

She understood. And when she told him about how she'd deployed her shelter, although it could tear him asunder to think of her alone and terrified again, fighting the heat and terror—the fact that she *had* deployed, that she hadn't frozen...a guy could almost breathe again.

She knew the costs and how to take care of herself, and besides, he planned on being with her every single jump this summer.

Which was why, perhaps, he'd let himself lean in, take her in his arms. Why today he wasn't slamming his head against a wall, the panic welling up to choke him. And why he couldn't get his mind off heading down to the parachute loft. Sure, if Miles found out, he might decide to put the kibosh on their new status. But this wasn't just a flashover summer romance.

This was Blazin' Kate Burns, the woman he'd never been able to extinguish from his heart.

In the main area, a half-eaten tuna fish sandwich lay in its open wrapper on the counter next to a large map that covered one wall, push-pins indicating fires both current and past around the nation. The hotshot team, including the veteran smokejumpers who had attached to it, had returned late last night. He'd risen to Pete and Reuben's gear piled in the family room, the husky scent of smoke rising from the pile of grimy clothing.

Miles returned in a moment, picking up the sandwich, chewing as he studied the board, a printout in his hand. Jed got up, wandered out to him. "What do you see?"

"There's a flare-up south of here, in the Bob Wilderness, but the Missoula jumpers are on it. And the West Yellowstone team is on a fire down in the Wind River Range. The McCall team went in to boost the Grangeville group down in the Seven Devils in Idaho." He took another bite of his lunch. "And we're just sitting around, reading magazines."

"The team needs a little R&R after this past week," Jed said. "And tonight is the graduation for the smokejumpers, so there's a party brewing."

Miles washed the last of his meal down with a Coke. "How many finished?"

"We have ten for sure, two more on the line." A line over which he didn't know if he should push them. In fact— "Is

Kate still in the loft?" He kept his voice cool, and it must have worked because Miles shrugged, crushed his can, and tossed it into the trash in a practiced basketball shot.

"Think so," he said, and leaned over their weather tech, eyes on the high and low pressure fronts dotting their way across the screen.

Jed left him there and, casually, his hands in his pockets, walked down the hall then into the ready room. At one of the long tables, their master rigger, Ruck Cameron, was folding a chute, the lines laid out, the canopy smoothed.

"Jed," he said in greeting. "I've pulled out every chute, and Kate's checking them over. The woman is driven."

"She watched one of her rookies take a swan dive, nearly hit the dirt. Yeah, I'd say she's driven," Jed said, clamping him on the back. Twenty years Ruck had invested in the packing game. Jed found it hard to believe he'd missed a rip in a canopy. Ruck apparently did too, because he shook his head.

"Some of these canopies are old, but I go through every one after a fire, make sure it's still sound. Can't figure how three of them ended up with tears."

"Three?"

"I know. Terrifying," he said, and nodded toward the tower, where parachutes hung from the ceiling like jellyfish. On the other side of the room, he could hear the whir of a Singer. "Kate is doing a little extra reinforcement."

A little? Jed turned and spotted Kate, a canopy laid out, two more wadded on the workbench. The rest of the chutes lay folded on the tables. He stood watching her as she bent over the machine, her hair plaited in two braids, held back with a blue bandana tied behind her head. She wore a yellow team T-shirt and her regulation canvas pants, a pair of Keens, and had caught her lip on her bottom teeth in concentration.

He could stand here all day waiting for the brilliant smile that could stop his world cold, restart it with a flush of heat and desire.

Wow, he loved her.

Loved. He hadn't let his feelings congeal into thought until now, but in truth he couldn't remember *not* loving her.

The realization swept through him, and in its wake, a tremble at how much he longed for them to find a way to live happily-ever-after in a world where a stiff wind could blow their lives apart.

He unleashed a steadying breath, shoved his hands into his pockets, and headed over to her.

She looked up, and he expected a smile. Instead— "Wait until you see what I found."

"That sounds ominous."

She finished stitching the row, pulled the fabric away, and snipped the ends of the threads. Then she got up and took his hand.

He was hoping for something a little more affectionate, but she dragged him over to the table. "So far I found three chutes with tears."

"Yeah, Ruck told me. That sounds...well, not okay, but these are old chutes—"

"I'm not talking regular wear and tear." She picked up a chute, searching through the yards of silken white fabric. She located her source, grabbed it, turning. "This is not a rip, Jed. This is a tear—a deliberate tear."

He took the fabric, examining the tear. A three-inch opening, about six inches from a seam.

"See how it's smooth, like it's been stabbed and pulled? The threads are seared clean off. If this had been a puncture, say from a tree, it would be jagged, the surrounding threads dangling. And wear usually happens around the seams, not in the middle of the fabric."

She put her hand over the hole, looked up at him. "This was deliberate."

He took a breath. "Kate—seriously. Yes, this looks like what you say, but think about it. Who would deliberately sabotage the chutes of a jump team?"

"Right? It's crazy." She took a long breath. "I don't know. But I've checked all the chutes, and only these three"—she indicated the two on the table, the one at her machine—"are damaged. And I also reinforced a few fraying seams on the others. We should be good to go, but I think we need to lock up the ready room and the loft when we're not here."

He had no words for that, or the insane idea that someone might want to hurt them.

"Maybe they got damaged after the fire last year. There were a lot of people upset—they could have been handled roughly."

She studied him for a moment, then her breath eased out. "Maybe. You're right—there was a lot of chaos at the end of the season. Who knows how—or by whom—these chutes were put away."

He took her hand, pressed it to his mouth. "Good thing you're here," he said, then drew her to himself. "We'll lock up the loft...in fact, I like that idea a lot..." He caught her chin in his hand, lowering his mouth for a kiss.

"Jed! What are you doing?" She pressed her hands to his chest, her voice cut low as she glanced over his shoulder at Ruck. "Not here."

He grinned and took her hand, pulling her toward the tower. "C'mon—no one will see us..."

"Jed—"

He glanced at Ruck, absorbed in his packing, and then pushed her into the tower and toward the frothy embrace of a white canopy, draping it around them. "I used to dream about this," he said, settling his hands on her hips. "I've always been a little crazy about you, Kate. From the first moment I met you and you looked up at me with those amazing green eyes. You always made me feel invincible."

He tugged on her braid, and her beautiful mouth answered in a grin.

"It was your laughter and the way you made everybody feel like they belonged—made *me* feel like I belonged. Every time I headed up to the Airstream to shoot the breeze with your dad, I was secretly hoping you'd wander out, sit with us under the stars. I'm not sure why, but you made me feel safe, Kate. Maybe it was the fact that I could see myself in your eyes—"

"Oh, I wasn't that easy, was I?"

He laughed. "You were. I could see you crushing on me for miles."

She covered her face. "I was so transparent."

He drew her hand away, kissed it. "It only made me like you more." He folded his fingers between hers. "I was always trying to figure out ways to talk to you without Jock knowing about it. In my worst nightmares he figured out the mad crush I had on you, too, and he beat me within an inch of my life. Or kicked me off the hotshots—I'm not sure what would have been worse."

"You're pretty tough. You could have taken the beating," she said, winking.

"Yeah, well, I can admit to a few scuffles with guys who might have had their eye on you. Like that guy Nate, from Sheridan. He practically followed you around the entire summer."

"He was cute. A cowboy—"

"He was a loose cannon. Walked off the line halfway through the summer. He didn't know how to stick around to the end."

"And you do?" She touched his cheek, running her finger down his face into the hollow of his neck, lighting a fire.

"Yeah," he said, his voice husky. He couldn't stop himself from leaning over, brushing her neck with his lips. "I do. Although I can admit this, here, was something I thought would never happen." He raised his head, caught her gaze. "I should have done this seven years ago," he said softly and bent down, pressing his lips to hers.

Now this was what he'd been thinking about, waiting for all day. The heady abandon of losing himself in Kate's smell, the taste of her, the little noise she made when he kissed her well, how she moved into him, molding herself to him.

It was Grizzly's and more. Much more, because this Kate was smarter, savvier. This Kate knew just how hard it was for him to let her go.

This Kate would be careful with his way-too-fragile heart.

She wove her hands up, around his neck, playing with the hair at his nape, stretching her body against his, her kiss languid and soft, lingering. It was all he could do not to skim his hands down her body, give in to the sudden racing of his heart.

But despite the fact Jock had departed from the earth, he still lingered in Jed's head. Enough for him to rein in his desire. For now.

Still, the longing turned every nerve ending to fire as he pressed his forehead to hers. "In my head, I dreamed of us fighting fires together, building a life in Ember. I might not have thought that through all the way, what that meant, but I always believed we belonged together, Kate."

She leaned back, her eyes shining. "We're going to be okay, aren't we? You're not going to freak out the next time I put on my jumpsuit, right?"

He kissed the tip of her nose. "How about if we talk about something else. Like whether we pass Hannah and Riley."

She frowned, just a little. "Jed, seriously—"

"I trust you, okay? You just need to trust me back. I'm going to keep my promise to do my best to not freak out, all right?"

She traced her finger down his cheek, freshly shaven this morning. "I think we need to pass them both."

"Really?" He put her away from him, just enough so that she didn't distract him with the feel of her body against his, the touch of her hands—although he couldn't run too far, not inside the tower. "I don't know..."

"Riley McCord has finally stopped thinking of this as a grand adventure. Getting rid of Paul helped. I think he can actually do this. And Hannah. She's wants this."

"She can barely make her landings," he said.

"But yesterday she didn't freak out when her reserve got knotted. She kept her cool."

"She had no choice," he said, wanting suddenly to forget the image of her struggling with the chute and how, for ten long seconds, he thought he might throw up in front of his recruits. And the thought of what he'd have to say to Ray...he shook the image away. That was why he remained detached—or tried to. So he could do his job. "I know she wants this, but—"

"She could have screamed and lost her head, even done something really stupid and cut away her reserve. But she didn't—she fought the knot and won."

"This time."

"Right. Well, we can only do what we can—I've examined all the chutes, Ruck is repacking them, and the rest we have to leave to faith that everyone will be okay."

"Really?"

She drew in a long breath, lifted a shoulder. "Trying on my dad's legacy. He always had it, you know—faith. Only time I saw it shaken was—"

"In Alaska."

"Right." She shook her head. "But he believed in a good outcome, and that's how he lived his life."

He wished he could see the benefit of that, really. But he couldn't rely on fate or hope or luck—or whatever faith looked like. "We can't pass someone who isn't ready."

She pressed her hand on his chest. "I wasn't ready."

He took a long breath, her hand burning where she'd touched him. "No, you weren't. But you had the look. And you...you had the instincts."

"Hannah does too. And yes, I'll probably lose my mind if anything happens to her, but I know what it feels like to work harder than every guy out there to prove yourself. To carry the weight and outthink the fire and basically make sure you don't endanger lives because you might be smaller, lighter, even weaker. Hannah deserves this."

He tipped up her chin, met those beautiful green eyes. "Just like you did."

A slow smile.

"Okay. We'll pass them both."

Kate curled her hand around his neck, brought his head down to meet her lips. This time, her kiss was anything but slow, anything but soft.

It only stirred the smolder inside. He let out a soft, guttural moan and grabbed her up, his arms around her waist, his heart thundering in his chest. Probably he should be thankful for the scant privacy the canopy afforded them.

His pulse raced hot in his head as he deepened his kiss. He put her down, and his hands moved lower—

She slowly put her hands on his and pulled them away. "Jed—"

"Sorry." His breath came out ragged. "Sorry." He pressed his forehead to hers. "I suddenly can't seem to get enough of you."

This elicited a smile as she wove her fingers into his. He was leaning down for another go when he heard a voice from the door.

"I know you're in there, Boss. And I get the feeling you're not alone, so whoops! Sorry about that. But even so, Miles wants to talk to you."

Jed froze. Pete. "Shoot—"

Kate grinned, leaned up, and kissed him.

He caught her shoulders, backed away. "Shh—Kate. This isn't—"

But she waggled her eyebrows and nipped at his lower lip.

"What are you *doing*?"

"Jed Ransom, Mr. Self-Control, seems to be in over his head."

He gave her a look. She pulled his arms behind her, leaned in.

"Stop it," he whispered. "Be quiet. Maybe he'll go away."

"He won't go away," Pete said, now walking into the room.

"It's Pete," she mouthed.

"I know," Jed mouthed back.

"Aw, C'mon, Jed. I swear, I won't tell anyone." More steps.

"Fine!" Jed grabbed the edge of the canopy and spilled it back to reveal Kate in his arms, giggling.

Pete, dressed in his green pants and a white T-shirt, stopped, mouth open. Then a small, playful grin lit his face. "I guess I need to send back the wedding invites."

Huh?

But Kate laughed, disentangling herself from Jed, from the canopy. She stepped away, just the slightest blush pressing her face.

"I told you, right?" Pete said to her, and she just shrugged, still smiling

"Told her what?" Jed said, glancing at her a second before heading for the door.

"Kate might want to hear this, too," Pete said, turning. "The fire investigators from Boise are here. They have a report on that drone we found at the Solomon River fire."

"Oh, yeah?" Kate turned, hot on his tail.

A woman dressed in the Bureau of Land Management browns waited for them in Miles's office, holding her iPad.

Jed stuck out his hand, introduced himself, Pete, and Kate.

"Amy Fee, out of the Inter-Agency Fire Center in Boise. It's good to see you again, Kate."

Jed glanced at Kate, remembering her days in Boise.

"Jeff and I just got back from the Solomon River site." Amy indicated another man, now striding down the sidewalk outside. "And from the burn pattern, as well as the remains of the flare, we have our suspicions that this fire was deliberately set." She pulled up a picture on her iPad. "If you'll look here at the fire source, you'll see a number of different fuels—grasses, kindling, a mound of materials that would flash over and keep burning until the suspect departed, but close enough to the campfire to make it look as if it might be accidental."

Kate was examining the picture. "What was this?"

"Like Jed said, it's the remains of what looks like a weather drone or a remote-control airplane."

"A kid's toy?"

"It seems bigger than that, more sophisticated."

"Did it crash?"

"It doesn't look like it—it seems more of a set fire. We'll bring the drone back to the lab and see what we can extract, but if there is someone setting fires out in the Kootenai, with weather conditions the way they are, well..."

Jed wanted to reach out, take Kate's hand.

"You'd better get your team ready, because you're in for a hot and lethal summer."

CHAPTER 8

SOMETHING HAD STOLEN THE corporeal form of Jed Ransom and replaced him with a warm and friendly— even devastatingly charming—double.

Not that Kate was complaining...really, but the sight of him holding Hannah Butcher's nephew, little Bucky Turnquist, did crazy things to her insides.

Turned them strangely warm and unwieldy.

The turnabout could leave her head spinning.

All afternoon, Jed seemed preoccupied. From the moment Amy had arrived with her dark news, through the setup of the graduation ceremony on the tarmac with the gleaming red-and-white Twin Otter as a backdrop, to the reception set up on folding tables in the hangar. Kate attributed it to the arson news, coupled with the canopy sabotage, but seeing him now, holding Bucky on his arm as if he'd been handling babies all his life...

"Adorable-man-holding-baby alert, twelve o'clock."

Gilly sidled up to her, handed her a chocolate chip cookie on a napkin. "It's enough to make a girl swoon."

Indeed.

Jed laughed, and the sound lifted from across the crowd and curled inside her, igniting a smolder. *I always believed we belonged together, Kate.*

She let a smile tip her lips.

"Oh my gosh—it's true." Gilly's tone made Kate glance
at her. Gilly wore a conspiratorial grin, shaking her head.
"When Pete said he'd found you two locking lips—"

"I'm going to kill him. He said he would keep it quiet." She glanced around for the rat, found him flirting—of
course—with a couple of unfamiliar town girls, probably rela-
tives of one of the graduates. As if sensing her ire, Pete looked
over at her.

She shook her head, her mouth a tight bud of disapprov-
al.

He frowned at her, as if, *what gives?*

Gilly saw the exchange and held up her hand as if to stop
him from stalking over to them, demanding explanation.
"What did you expect? I think the guy really did carry a little
torch for you. He came into the hangar and plopped down on
the sofa with a big sigh like his heart was breaking."

"Hardly."

"He mentioned a duel at dawn with pistols," Gilly said,
and Kate laughed. "No seriously, he did come in with a
strange look on his face, but it took Reuben's prodding to get
it out of him. And he swore us to secrecy."

Pete still wore a frown, glancing at her now and again,
and Kate put him out of his misery with a shake of her head
and a smile. She rolled her eyes, and the dour look broke free.

"So...you and Jed, round two?" Gilly said. "For the record, you look good on him. I've never seen the man so
cheery in all my years."

Really? Kate glanced again at him, this time catching
Jed holding little Buck like a football, swinging him gently
as he talked with Ray, Hannah's father. She swallowed back a

flush of emotion at the way he filled out his uniform, the fact that those amazing arms had been wrapped around her, those strong hands twined into her hair and caressing her face.

"You don't think that he'd...well, he said he'd had a thing for me for years, too," she said quietly to Gilly. "He wouldn't do something crazy, like—"

"What—propose?"

And Kate just stopped breathing.

"Kate—Kate, come back to me." Gilly snapped her fingers in front of Kate's face. "I was kidding. Sorta. I mean, why not? You've loved him since you were fifteen. He's probably loved you for that long, too, if he were to admit it. You guys were made for each other. So?" She lifted her shoulder, turned her gaze deliberately back to Jed. "When's the wedding?"

"Stop. Talking. Please. Stop talking."

Gilly laughed. "Now who's the one making a run for the hills?"

Kate managed a tight smile, but as Gilly moved away to congratulate another graduate, she saw Jed, lying in the hospital bed so many years ago, not a little panic on his face when she arrived in his room wearing her heart on the outside of her body, ready to hand it over.

She turned and nearly ran right into Riley McCord, who had planted himself in front of her, looking official and serious in his uniform, the blue Forest Service Jump patch pinned to his shirt. "Thanks for passing me, Kate." The cockiness she'd noticed three weeks ago had vanished from his eyes, replaced by a pride, a confidence she wished she could feel.

She gripped his shoulder, met his gaze. "Don't let me down." He nodded and moved away just in time for her to see Jed hand the baby back to Ray. Then Jed turned and seemed to be searching—yeah, for her, because when he spotted her, a smile lit his face, his eyes warming.

And she melted under it, her heart reacting to being on the receiving end of all that Jed Ransom focus. She couldn't move, her body paralyzed as he worked through the crowd toward her, glad-handing graduates and family members, clamping some on the shoulder, his smile a thousand watts of stun power, even to the casual victim.

She had to get out of here before he did something crazy like—

"Hey, everyone. I'd like your attention, if I could." He stopped in the center of the crowd, raised his hand, his voice. The hum of the attendees dimmed for him, people turning.

"I just wanted to take this opportunity to say a few words about someone who changed my life. Fifteen summers years ago I landed on this person's doorstep and set out on a journey to become someone who was worthy of that person's admiration. That person's respect."

He smiled at the crowd and held up his cup. Kate wrapped her arms around herself. She caught Pete's eye, and he shrugged. Gilly was grinning over the top of her glass.

No, he couldn't...

"It's a new season and a time for new beginnings."

She edged back even as Jed's gaze roamed the crowd.

It settled on her, and he smiled, sweetly, not a hint of danger in his expression.

No, Jed—she tried to put the words in her gaze, on her face.

"Which is why today I want to raise a glass to the men who have gone before us. To Jock Burns and the smokejumpers and hotshots who made us proud, who still teach us every day the meaning of heroism and commitment. Who believe that what they do matters."

Oh. Kate hadn't realized she'd been holding her breath—and let it out in a sound of relief highly inappropriate for the moment. She clamped her hand over her mouth, raised her lemonade to the applause.

Silly woman. Of course he wouldn't—

Oh boy. Because he was making his way over to her again, looking whole and contented. She swallowed back the sense of her world tilting and smiled back. "That was a nice toast."

He put his arm around her shoulders. Squeezed. She glanced around to see who might be looking and found only Conner's gaze on them. He wore an enigmatic look, bordering on a frown, and it had her turning away, confused.

"I have to schmooze with a few more of the locals, then what do you say we get out of here?" Jed asked, leaning down to whisper in her ear.

She nodded and he moved away. She glanced at Conner again, but he'd turned his back to her and she shook away his look as her own crazy apprehensions.

So what, the entire base might know about them. She knew of plenty fire-base romances that ignited over the summer. Although maybe that was the problem. Maybe Conner saw her flying away at the end of the season, back to Boise. Or Alaska. And, being Jed's friend, knew how Jed might feel about that.

She hadn't thought beyond coming home, sorting out her dad's possessions, living in the Airstream, becoming the jump trainer, and overcoming the fear that had held her hostage for so long.

Funny, she hadn't woken up with nightmares for over two weeks, ever since...since Jed first kissed her at the Solomon fire. Since she'd stepped back into his airspace, since she knew, despite her protests, that she wasn't alone.

Then last night—it all happened so quickly, this turn-around, and suddenly he was talking about something beyond summer...

In my head, I dreamed of us fighting fires together, building a life in Ember.

Now, the sun hung lazily over the horizon, the oppressive heat of the day lifting in a fragrant, piney breeze. Kate walked over to the shadow of the Twin Otter, to the podium and the almost empty audience chairs.

Gemma Turnquist sat on the end of the front row, ram-rod straight, staring at the plane like she'd seen a ghost. Kate walked closer, not sure if she should intrude—but a catch of breath, the glisten of tears on Gemma's face made her stop.

Kate pivoted, turning to leave when, "Someday, you'll have to make a choice, you know."

She froze. Looked over her shoulder. Gemma still stared straight ahead, as if she hadn't spoken. But, "If you love him, you'll have to choose."

Kate turned fully, blew out a breath. "Uh, are you talking to me?"

"Either you or Jed. And in the end, both of you." She looked over at her, then, a tear dripping off her chin, her face bullet hard. "Jed acts like it's all glamour and heroics, but it's not. It's a choice—fire or family. My husband chose fire."

"Gemma—"

"No. I get it. I mean, how can a pregnant wife compete with the camaraderie of eight guys all flinging themselves out of an airplane to fight a dragon? It's practically medieval." Her expression turned livid. "But it's hardly heroic."

Another tear dripped from her jaw, and she looked back at the plane as if seeing her husband hanging out of the door, ready to jump. "Doug always said it was in his blood. That he was born to jump—and Hannah has swallowed that line whole. The entire lot of them, drinking the Kool-Aid, believing that it's a family legacy, that they're born to it, that they have no choice." She closed her eyes. "Apparently it's also a family legacy to drive your family crazy with worry and even leave behind a widow and a child who will never know his father—"

"Gem—"

She held up a trembling hand. "Don't, Kate. You're the worst of them."

Kate flinched.

"You make them believe they have to be braver. Stronger. Tougher than the daughter of the great and mighty Jock Burns." She flung out her arm, gesturing to the unseen crowd. "Every single one of those guys longs to impress you. And because of that, they'll do something stupid." Her eyes narrowed, her voice sharp and thin. "If they come home in body bags, it'll be your fault."

Kate blinked at her, nonplussed. "You've got to be kidding me. I'm just doing what—"

"You love. I get it. You were *born* to this, right?"

Um. "Yeah." She took a breath, her head spinning at Gemma's words. "Listen—since I was a kid, it's all I wanted to do. And yeah, it's a legacy thing. My dad—"

"I know. Filled your brain with stories of danger and heroism."

"My dad practically forbade me to jump! He heard about it and went ballistic and begged me not to jump!"

And she'd made it worse by walking out of his life. The rawness of that truth could level her. Oh, her pride—her selfish pride. But what choice did she have now?

Her voice fell. "But I walked away from him, and if I

don't jump, Gemma, then I've got nothing. I *am* nothing. This is it, right here. Everything I am. Everything I will ever be. A smokejumper."

Kate wasn't sure where the words came from, surprised at the heat of them and the moisture that burned her eyes. Her chest rose and fell, her voice shaky. "I'm not going to get anyone killed, Gemma. These guys are here because they want to be—and they deserve to be. They've worked hard—"

"And Hannah. My *sister*. Does she deserve to be here?"

Kate drew in a breath. Tightened her jaw. Nodded. "Yeah. She does."

Gemma stared at her without speaking. Just her eyes, tough, daring, in Kate's. Then she got up, lifted her chin. "Hannah has more than this. She has a family, a life. A future. Don't make her into you."

She strode up to her. "And don't let her die."

The "or else" hung there, or maybe Kate just imagined it. Gemma took a final breath then strode past her.

Kate turned, watching her go, her entire body vibrating with Gemma's grief. Her gaze fell on a figure standing in the shadows, his hands in his pockets, his face grim.

Jed.

Gemma walked by him without a glance.

He watched her go then looked back at Kate. Took a breath. "You have nothing?"

Her throat burned with the echo of her words. *Oh.* "Jed—what do you want from me? I've never lied to you, never made you think that I could be the girl who would settle down. You see where I live—I'm a rental-house, Air-stream-camper, jump-in-my-Jeep-and-drive-to-the-next-great-fire kind of girl."

He blew out a breath, lowering his head, as if in pain. His

shoulders rose, fell.

Shoot. She came toward him. "Jed—listen to me—I love you—I think you know that. But—"

"It's not enough." He looked up then and met her eyes, something broken in his. "I should have seen it all along." His face twisted in a sort of wry, sad expression. "Yeah, you might love me, but you also love fire."

He shook his head as if, wow, how stupid he'd been.

The gesture put a fist over her heart.

"I do—I'm just like my dad—"

"Yeah, babe, you are—but not in the way you think. You think your legacy is that Jock could face fire without fear. But it's not. Your dad's legacy was *Ember*. The Jude County firefighters—people like me, who he practically raised, and the men and women he trained. Your dad spent his entire life building the thing you love the most about fighting fire— camaraderie. Maybe he figured it out after your mom left, I don't know. But your dad didn't love fire—he loved the people who fought it."

She clenched her jaw against the tightening of her throat.

"Your dad died because he ran into a fire to save the people he loved."

His eyes were so earnest, she couldn't move.

"And you got it too, Kate, without even knowing it. The recruits love *you*—not your legacy. But you can't see it, because you're too busy running after the next great fire. And I just figured out why. It's not so you can prove yourself— you've already done that. It's because you're scared."

"I'm not scared," she said, but her voice shook. How did he—

"Not of fire." His face twitched then. "You're scared of this. Us. Of jumping in and being betrayed. Which is why building a life with me has you completely freaked out. Because that would mean you would have to stop running and actually stick around and face your greatest fear—that one day it could all implode, just like it did for your parents. And it's easier to blame fire and legacy and this inane idea that you have to shake a fist at death to prove yourself. That's easier than facing the terrifying thought that you could have something amazing and beautiful, only to have it turn to ash."

The fist closed over her heart, squeezed.

"Embracing that would take real courage, wouldn't it, Kate?" His eyes glistened. "And you just don't have the guts to face *that* kind of risk, do you? A home, a family. And the scariest thing of all—a happy ending."

And there it was. The rawness of everything he wanted, right there in his eyes—a home, a family. Everything he'd never gotten but after all these years was still holding out hope for.

With her.

The vision reached out, right down to her soul, and shook her.

Yeah, maybe she *was* afraid. Because as much as fire scared her, she understood it, even though it could turn on her.

It was safer to face the dragon she knew than to stand there with her heart in her hands, handing it over for Jed to crush.

Again.

She had no reserve chute for that scenario.

But apparently, he wasn't finished. "You talk about having faith—you used to have it, Kate. You were the girl who made me look up into the heavens and believe there was Someone looking back. I so envied you. You and your Dad had this faith and courage, and I went over to your place not only to see you but because you and Jock made me believe in God's protection, His providence. Sheesh—you had me practically convinced. And when you sang after the fire in Alaska, I thought—yeah. God was there. He was watching over us. And then you just walked away. You just turned your back on all of us, including God."

The words boiled up in her chest, came out in a low hiss. "I didn't leave God, Jed. He left *me*. I prayed and prayed that you'd live. And it worked—you lived. And then you pushed me away. And Dad—I thought he'd be proud of me. But no—he looked at me and said God wasn't my parachute. And it's true, because then...even God left me. Alone. To burn on the hill in Idaho. So yeah, it's just me, Jed. Just me. Because, guess what—you told me to Get. Out. Of. Your. Life!"

"I lied!" His voice rose, trembling, and beyond him, she saw a few heads turn. But he seemed past caring. "I was freakin' terrified. We both nearly died, and I couldn't let that happen again—"

"Well, you were pretty convincing. And what was I supposed to do? You—my dad. Both of the men I—" She cut her words off. "You both wanted me to quit. You both made me *choose*. So I did."

"And do you blame us?" His eyes blazed. "Of *course* I don't want you to jump. How insane is it to love someone you know could die? But I do anyway, because I'm not stupid enough to think that I'm going to stop you. And I know that I jump to—but I'm sorry, I can't get it out of my head that one of these days your chute isn't going to open, or you're going to blow into a flare-up, or maybe just get trapped again, and this time, burn to death. And those thoughts can paralyze me. I'm just holding onto the wild, desperate—yeah, okay, faith—that you won't get hurt. That you'll be smart out there, and that by some grace that I don't deserve, you'll come back to me."

He looked away then, shook his head. Back to her, his eyes wet. "Except, clearly, I'm lying to myself, because I get it now—you'll never really belong to me as long as you belong to fire."

She wiped her cheek and her voice dropped, thin. "You *don't* get it, Jed. Mom broke him. I heard him crying—my dad *crying*—in his bunk. And I vowed I'd never let someone destroy me like that."

"So you made smokejumping your god, your lover, your life. And there's no room in there for me or any future we hoped to have."

"I didn't make you any promises, Jed."

"No, you didn't. I should have noticed that, but maybe I'm like my dad in that way, because I believe too hard in something that will never happen. You might call that faith, but I call it being a fool."

He turned, and she thought he was going to walk away. But then he stopped. "And for the record—I could probably come to accept you fighting fire if I knew you could see that you had a very good reason to stay alive."

She stood, stunned, holding her empty lemonade cup, his words poisoning her to stillness.

He cut through the crowd, managing a stiff smile to a few recruits, then stalked out to the parking lot.

She watched him pull out and leave the party in a cloud of dust and gravel.

Jed sat on an Adirondack chair on the back deck of his house, holding a Coke, tracing the misty trail of the Milky Way, swallowing back the burn in his throat, reliving every single word, every nuance of their fight.

"Jed—listen to me—I love you—I think you know that. But—"

And now he wanted to pound his fist against something, or better yet, his head, maybe knock free the foolish thought that she might, yes, stay here and build a life—with him.

He knew better. Oh, he knew much, much better.

"Jed—what do you want from me? I've never lied to you, never made you think that I could be the girl who would settle down. You see where I live—I'm a rental-house, Airstream-camper, jump-in-my-Jeep-and-drive-to-the-next-great-fire kind of girl."

He took another drink and winced. He'd turned out *exactly* like his dad. Gambling, throwing faith after something that could never happen.

He heard the front door open, steps across the house, into the kitchen. Then the squeal of the screen door and the deck boards groaning.

Conner settled in on the chair beside him. Unlaced his boots.

Silence.

"How much did you hear?"

"Let's see. Everything from you blaming Kate for your lack of faith to telling her that she was a fool for doing what she loves. Calling her afraid. And then there was the part where you nearly blew out a tire driving away. Pretty exciting evening, I have to say."

"You can leave."

"Mmmhmm. Nope. Because misery loves company." He leaned back, staring at the sky, toeing off his boots. "And, like you, I just have my empty, lonely trailer to go home to, and I'd rather sit here with you and try and figure out why the women we love don't want us."

Oh.

"Although, in your case, I have some idea."

Jed shot him a look. Conner didn't spare him a glance.

They fell silent, the sounds of the night weaving around them—the wind across the tall grasses, the scent of lupine and wild roses, and far away the hum of some band at the Hotline, the after party kicking up for the graduates.

"She loves fire more than me. What am I supposed to do with that?"

"Nothing. Let her do her job. Which, by the way, you'll have to start doing if you want to be a leader instead of a lovesick boy."

"Hey—!"

"I didn't see you tackling Pete when the slurry rained down on us. Just sayin'"

"She could have gotten hurt."

"Yes. She could have, and yes, you can protect her as a teammate. But you can't save her from chance—accidents happen on a fire line. It's unpredictable."

"Unless you stay one step ahead."

"It's going to catch up with you, bro."

Like it did Jock. Jed sighed. "I know. You only have to be unlucky once. I wish I could get her to see that."

"You thought that you could win Kate's heart, make her choose you over smokejumping?"

"No. Or yes. I don't know. I *do* know that I'm done trying to protect her. I was a fool to think I could change her, show her she doesn't have to be afraid to—"

"Love you? Because that's what this is about, isn't it? Just like her mom, you're asking her to choose."

"I'm just trying to protect her from herself."

"Wow. I knew you thought highly of yourself, but—"

"Seriously, you can leave."

"Bro, think about it. Let's say that she does choose you. Is that truly loving her?"

"If it keeps her alive."

"So love is making someone do what you want?"

"I didn't ask her to quit!"

"She's not stupid."

He closed his eyes. "Fine. Okay. Someday, maybe. But that's a long way off—"

"You hovering all the way to the bitter end. And tell me how that would work out for the both of you."

Jed finished off his Coke. Crushed the can. "Okay, Romeo, tell me what to do."

"Trust me, if I had the answers, I wouldn't be sitting here on your deck with you. I'd be..." He sighed. "Well, not here."

Jed glanced at him, saw Conner's face had hardened into a dark glower.

"But I think love has to do a little bit with faith," Conner finally said.

"Give it a rest already."

"Hear me out. Faith that the other person wants to be with you, and that if you let them go a little bit, you leave room for surprises. For that moment when everything you hoped for is realized—and it had nothing to do with you arranging it, or controlling it, or planning it out, but trusting in that magic that happens when we let go and love takes over. That's faith—leaving room for miracles."

"I don't believe in miracles."

"Well, there's your problem. You rule out the impossible,

and all that's left is you trying to figure it out. That's way too much responsibility. You need to give God the chance to show up."

"And if He doesn't?"

"I think, if you're honest, God's already shown you that He will."

Jed drummed his fingers on his chair.

"Faith believes that God is on our side, every time, all the time, and that yes, He will show up," Conner said.

"He might be on your side. But not for guys like me. We gotta work for every break we get."

"Because you're not enough?"

Jed lifted a shoulder. "I'm not whining. I'm just stating a truth. I've always been in second place. I wasn't enough for my father to quit gambling, my uncle to quit drinking. Second always to something bigger, something that could destroy them...Yeah, it all adds up to me being nothing to any of them. And that's the problem. Faith assumes that someone is looking out for you and wants the best for you. Faith is the expectation that someone else is reaching back. But if you are always less than, if you're nothing, then why would anyone want to reach for you? The truth is you have to believe in God's love for you if you want to have faith, and there's just no reason for God to love me."

And wow, he didn't realize how much his chest would ache with those words.

Conner shook his head. "You've got the same virus Kate has—believing you have to prove yourself to God in order for Him to love you. It's done been proven, pal. God loves you enough to *already* save you. You just have to believe it, want it, embrace it."

The acid filled his throat. "God hasn't shown up in my

life since the day He rescued me and Kate from the fire. Believe me, I've looked...I'm nothing to Him."

Jed tossed his Coke can in a perfect arc to the trash bin just outside the deck. It hit and careened off into the grass.

"Jock didn't think you were nothing—in fact, he thought you were more than enough," Conner said, getting up to fetch the Coke can. He dropped it in the trash. "Have you ever stopped to wonder why he sent you to Alaska to train Kate all those years ago?"

"Because he wanted me to stop her."

Conner gave a laugh that conveyed no humor. "Please. He knew her better than you did. Do you think, for one moment, he harbored the serious thought that she'd quit?"

"He asked her to stop jumping."

"So did you. Did you expect a yes?"

"I—" No...Actually. And that hit him, hard. He drew in a breath. "He just wanted her to know he loved her, that he wanted her to be careful."

"And if my only daughter was going to do something so dangerous she might die, I'd handpick the person to train her. And if that person was in love with her, all the better to look out for her."

He winced. "I failed him."

"Hmmm. I thought you saved her life."

"She wouldn't have been there if I hadn't passed her in the first place."

Conner came back onto the deck, leaned against the railing, arms akimbo.

"Right. *That* season. But imagine the next season, she's back, and this time, you're not around. And maybe she does fine, but you can't draw a fire line around her, expecting to keep her safe forever. She *is* her father's daughter. Jock sent the one person to her who loved her as much as he did. That he knew would do the best for her—train her well, watch her back. He had faith in you and in your love for her. And here's a question for you—even though it didn't turn out like you'd hoped, even though she walked away from you, have you ever stopped thinking about her? For one day?"

Conner had him there.

"And Jock—he prayed for her, he asked about her. I know that he even sent a booster team in to Idaho to help a couple summers ago—I was on it. So, even though it seemed to her that you two didn't care, that was the farthest thing from the truth."

Jed nodded.

"You might consider that our perspective on our circumstances is a poor indicator of the bigger picture. She is not nothing to you. You are not nothing to God."

Jed stared at the stars winking at him, as if they might be listening.

"God didn't leave you to yourself, Jed. He sent Jock. I can't tell you how many times people asked him if you were his son. I know, because I was there. We'd just come off that fire in Minnesota—remember, with your buddy Darek? Jock had stayed behind to run a small fire out here. We were unwinding, playing darts, and in you walked. He walked over, in front of the entire crowd, and gave you a hug."

A smile worked up Jed's face, the memory swift and sweet. "I remember that." *Jock, I miss you.*

"You weren't nothing to him. And you're not nothing to Kate. She's just scared of losing everything she is. And you're not making it easier. Back up, let go. I didn't realize you two had finally—well, it's about time. But I know you, and I'll bet you had you two halfway to the altar."

"Oh, I was way beyond that, well into the honeymoon," Jed said, matching Conner's grin. "Yeah, okay. I might have conjured up a few plans for us." He a made a fist, tapped it on the arm of his chair. "Now...I don't know." He leaned his head back. "I don't know anything."

"I do, bro. I know that God loves you. And that He's not interested in obeying your plans. He's interested in giving you the best. And all you need to do is believe that. When you know God loves you, then faith is simply the expectation that God will show up, that love in hand."

"I'm losing her, Conner. Again."

"No. You never had her, not really. But you might, if you make room for miracles."

CHAPTER 9

For ONCE, KATE WOULD admit that Jed was completely, absolutely right.

She stood in the bedroom of her Airstream, her clothes strewn on her bed fighting the great and terrible urge to shove it all in the back of her Jeep and floor it. Head south to Missoula and the smokejumper team where her father's reputation could land her an interview, if not a job. Or maybe she should just head north, back to Alaska.

By now they'd be short staffed with a few injuries...

She picked up a pair of socks wadded in a ball, hearing Jed's caustic words. *And you just don't have the guts to face that kind of risk, do you? A home, a family. And the scariest thing of all—a happy ending.*

She threw the sock ball the length of the camper. It hit the rounded glass windows, just in time for her to see Gilly recoil, peer in, and stare at her.

Of course her best friend, the one who knew her history with Jed, would come to help her nurse her wounds. Kate didn't bother to wait for Gilly to knock. "Come in already."

She stared at the clothing on her bed, not sure if—or how—to hide her gut reaction to their fight.

And then it didn't matter, because Gilly came in and

plopped a plastic bag on the counter. "Red Velvet ice cream and hot fudge. They didn't have mint chocolate chip—this is the best I could do. Oh my—did we have a fight with our laundry? Or..." Her expression caught up to the evidence, her mouth opening. "Oh Kate, you're not thinking of leaving, are you?"

"Grab a couple spoons," Kate said, and Gilly rooted around in the utensil drawer as Kate unscrewed the hot fudge jar. She stuck it in the microwave while Gilly peeled back the lid on the ice cream box. Gilly stuck the spoon in her mouth, bowl down. "What happened? Did he commit the unforgivable sin and propose?"

"You here all week? Because I don't see a tip jar."

"That one's for free, because I'm still trying to understand. The parts I heard sounded like he was offering to settle down with you, start a family—yeah, he definitely deserves a kick in the knees." She handed Kate the container. "Are we eating this straight out of the carton?"

Kate lifted two bowls from the cupboard. "Apparently, Jed thinks I'm afraid of being happy, that I'd rather run away like a peeved teenager every time someone tells me something I don't want to hear."

Silence as Gilly dished up the ice cream.

"Gilly, that's not fair."

"I didn't say anything." She dug into the ice cream, taking a bite. "Your temper tantrums did make excellent fodder for some awesome adventures."

Kate scooped out the ice cream, not smiling. "Jed said that I was scared of being betrayed."

"Who isn't?"

"He said I love fire more than him."

Gilly put the spoon down. "Wow. Okay, I didn't realize

we had *that* fight." She touched Kate's arm. "I'm so sorry."

She sighed. "He said I'd never be his when I belonged to fire. And that I'd rather keep looking for the next epic fire than stick around and face the danger of loving him."

Gilly cast a look at the jeans, sweatshirts, running clothes, and the one pair of high heels tossed on the double bed. "Now he's just talking crazy."

Kate's mouth tightened as she poured the hot fudge over the ice cream. "He just couldn't get the fact that I was born to this. Smokejumping is in my DNA."

Silence.

"Gil?"

"I don't know. I was just thinking. What if...what if you only just *wanted* to be like your dad? I do remember ballet class."

"Are you kidding me? Ballet was my mother's pitiful attempt to get me to stop hanging around the fire camp." Kate scooped out another spoonful of ice cream. "You, on the other hand..."

Gilly gave a half smile, something of sadness in it. "Yeah, well, my ballet days are long over, unless you include aerobatics."

"In an Air Tanker?"

"Exactly." Gilly picked up her bowl, and Kate gestured to the front door. The evening air had cooled with the leaving of the sun, a scant humidity gathering in the grasses, and with it a breathy nip lifting the hair on her neck. Her bare feet chilled against the boards of the deck. She slid onto the picnic table, her gaze falling to Jed's house. Dark.

Gilly sat next to her. "But the ballet thing only brings up a point. You were different before your mom left. Happy. Girly, even. I remember thinking—what would it be like to be an only child? I was so jealous of you. I remember we'd be in church, and I'd be squished between Abe and Colt or next to Jake, trying to get him to stop pinching me. You'd be across the aisle with your dad and mom and I'd be thinking—what must it be like to be the center of all that love? And then, you lost it. Just like that—your mom walked away and started a new life, without you. Of course it changed you, Kate. I might be a little skittish of getting hurt, too."

Kate let the ice cream dissolve in her mouth. "I was always a little worried that my dad regretted taking me in. Here I was, underfoot all the time. He had to ask your dad to take care of me when he got called out, and when he came home, I'd be there, bugging him with questions and details and...I just wanted him to be glad that I stayed with him. I can agree I went into smokejumping to make him proud of me." She stirred her ice cream. "I never in a million years dreamed he'd be so angry." She took a bite, let the spoon linger on her tongue, remembering.

"He was so—undone when he came to Alaska after the fire. He came right out to the hospital, stormed in, and practically took me apart, right in front of Jed. I was mortified. I thought he was going to grab me by the arm and drag me home."

She took another bite, hearing his words, seeing his distraught expression. *God isn't a parachute!*

"He was pretty scared."

She glanced at Gilly. "I see that now."

Gilly nodded, gave her a wry smile. "Only took seven years."

Kate put down her ice cream, traced a falling star that unlatched from the sky. "I should have come home earlier. You have no idea how I regret that. But I...I was angry and embarrassed. And fueled by this insane need to prove him wrong. I only saw all that fury as rejection, not as love." She wiped a hand across her wet cheek. "I probably should have stopped, taken another look."

"You're not running now."

"Only because you brought ice cream," Kate said, not entirely kidding. She dipped her spoon back in. "Jed overheard me tell Gemma Turnquist that if I didn't have smokejumping, then I didn't have anything."

"Oh. So that's what the call to bravery was."

Kate glanced at her.

"Jed said something like, if you stuck around, that would be a real act of courage." Gilly held up her hands. "Hey, I was trying not to listen, but I thought someone should tune in, in case you needed a replay."

"I don't need a replay. He was furious, hurt, and basically called me a coward. But he doesn't get watching your parents' marriage unravel, seeing your mother walk away, your dad retreat into himself."

"So you stop Jed from hurting you before it begins, is that it?"

Kate shrugged.

"For a woman who likes to take risks—yeah, I think Jed's right. You're afraid."

"I'm not—" She sighed. "Okay, yeah. The fact is, yes, I want it, okay? Everything Jed had unspoken in his eyes. The home. The family. The guy. Jed. I want it all—but—"

"You're afraid to reach for something that could burn you."

Kate pursed her lips, shrugged. "All I know is that I thought I was born to jump fire. Then, suddenly, everything turned on me. The fire, Jed, Dad...and even God did it. Do you know how rare it is to have to deploy your fire shelter?

There are some firefighters who spend their entire careers without deploying it once. And me—twice. What does that tell you about God's love for me?"

"It tells me He's pretty crazy about you."

Kate stared at her. "Are you serious?"

"Kate—think about it. You've got this all backwards. Yes, you got trapped by a fire—twice. And. You. Lived. *Lived.* There are smokejumpers who say that the only good reason for a fire shelter is so that they can identify your body, that you can have an open casket. People don't live through fires—even in fire shelters. But you did. Twice. Wake *up.* I'm not sure how God can be *more* on your side."

Kate closed her eyes against a rush of thick emotion.

"God loves you, Kate. You just don't want to admit it. Because if you admit God is on your side, then you might have to admit that you *haven't* done this alone. That you need help—and that, right there, is a killer. Because then you aren't Blazin' Kate Burns, but rather just regular old Kate needing God like everyone else. And if God is with you on the mountain, then He'll be with you in—dare I say it?—marriage."

"I'm not afraid to need God."

"Are you kidding me? Of course you are. Because if you need God, then suddenly you have to listen to God. And if you listen, He might tell you something you don't want to hear. Like—swallow your stupid pride, go and reconcile with the man you should be with."

Or reconcile with your father.

Her throat burned.

"But here's the kicker—even if God asks you to do something hard. Like forgive. Or even—horrors—give up something you love for something bigger, it's because He wants you to succeed! All this time, you've been thinking God is like your father—ready to turn on you. But God is *for* you, Kate. He is on your side. And any warning flags He waves— like, perhaps, your father or Jed—is not meant to steal your dreams but help them come true. I'm not trying to break your heart here, but what if you had stuck around, let your dad teach you his tricks? Pass along his jump boss hat to you?"

Kate looked away, her eyes slick.

"I love you, Kate—and I'm not trying to hurt you. But that guy over there"—she pointed to Jed's dark house—"he's your dad's protégé, and I can guarantee that he is just as miserable as you are. He loved your dad. *You* loved your dad. And you love each other. I think the last thing you should be doing is sitting over here cooling off with ice cream when you should be over there, rekindling that fire."

Down the road, across the fire base, Jed's porch light flicked on, and she saw the front door open. Her heart gave a traitorous leap until she saw Conner's truck back out of the driveway.

"He thinks I take too many risks. That I'm stubborn and refuse to ask for help. He thinks I run away when someone stands in my way, go off and do my own thing and, most of all, that I don't want to build a life with him. I don't think he wants to have anything to do with me, Gilly."

"Oh, Kate. If anyone can prove Jed Ransom wrong, it's you."

Kate let Gilly's words sink in, settle into her bones.

"The question is, do you have the courage to face the fire? Because that's what love is—consuming, mesmerizing, exhilarating, terrifying, complex, and amazing." Gilly got up, turned to her, her voice soft enough to heal the bruises. "The good news, Blazin' Kate, is that nobody understands fire behavior like you do. Right?"

She left Kate sitting on the table watching the stars fall

behind the outline of Jed's once-again dark house.

"This is it, gents—and ladies."

Jed nodded at his team, his gaze landing on Hannah and Kate, leaning against the table in the back of the room where the maps of the Kootenai National Forest denoted the latest fire call, a flare up in Powder Canyon. He'd spent the better part of the last fifteen minutes mapping out the area, comparing the terrain with the Doppler, the infrared geo-satellite images, and the latest weather reports.

"This is the one we've been training for. We're dropping into ten acres of heavy black spruce, one-hundred percent active and rolling through a canyon toward an RV park, a resort, and not a few fishing lodges. Air Attack will be supporting us with at least one Air Tanker. We'll roll one load of jumpers, the second will stand by."

Jed scanned his clipboard, debating just a moment before he focused on the list. He read off Kate's name without inflection, right after his.

Some habits he couldn't break.

"Second load, wait for my order." Jed tucked the clipboard back on the duty wall, next to the roster, the hours logged, along with the names and status of the hotshots. He told Miles to put the shots on standby for possible mop-up, if not deployment for attack. But with the route into the fire at least two hours by camp road, the jumpers had a better chance of cutting off the fire before it got out of hand.

"Wheels up in fifteen," he said, and the crew dispersed. He caught Conner by the arm. "Bring your drone," he said. "This is a good fire to give it a try."

"Good idea, Boss."

Conner's newest invention—a fire drone—could fly over the fire and, in the right conditions, measure fuels, wind speed, and fire behavior, give them more eyes, a better battle strategy.

Twenty minutes later, Gilly lifted them off, and Jed positioned himself with his map, binoculars, and radio in the front of the plane, next to Cliff O'Dell, again spotting for them. The sun hung in the sky, blotted by a few bulbous, angry gray clouds, more bluster than potency. He leaned back, tried not to glance at Kate, thinking through his plan of fire attack.

She'd shown up for roll call this morning as if they hadn't had a spinout yesterday—all smiles, *Yes, Sirs* and *Right Away, Boss,* and it had him unbalanced.

He'd expected ire, a cold shoulder, and, at the very least, a bucking of his leadership when he didn't move her up to squad boss for the jump.

Instead, she sat in the back of the plane next to Hannah, shouting into her ear, although her words didn't carry to his position. Hannah laughed, Kate smiled, and it turned the knife in his chest.

You never had her, not really. But you might, if you make room for miracles.

Jed looked out the window at the blanket of black spruce, lodgepole pine, and the rolling mountains and canyons, the glacier rivulets that scarred the land. The hum of the prop wash filled his ears.

A tap on his arm and Cliff pointed into the canyon to a deep, gray-blue wall of frothy smoke, rolling over itself as it bubbled up from tongues of flame. Jed guesstimated the flame lengths at maybe twenty to thirty feet at the head, making a run toward a river at the base of a canyon.

The plane offered him a decent view of the ten acres, the

way the fire settled into a crevice at the bottom of the canyon along a seasonal creek bed to the east, rising from the cauldron to lick up the edges toward a towering western ridge. A hiking trail ran across the top edge of the ridge, a feeble but possible fire break if they couldn't get the blaze to calm down before it climbed the mountain.

By the way the wind was blowing down the canyon, away from the ridge, it seemed the smarter attack was on the eastern side, to lay down retardant against the dry creek bed. They could use it as a boundary, snuff out any spurs, and drive the fire toward the river. Jed made a mental note to suggest it to Air Attack.

"Hold on to your reserves!" Cliff yelled and opened the jump door. He had already clipped into the overhead line and now stuck his head into the slipstream, searching for a jump site.

Cliff ducked his head back in. "You've got your work cut out for you!" he shouted to Jed. "If you can stop it along the riverbed, you have a chance of containing it in the canyon. Keep an eye on the winds. This fire is creating its own weather." He leaned back out and dropped streamers, watching as two got sucked into the blackened smoke.

The plane jostled against the turbulent wind currents, a product of flying through the boiling ash. Cliff dropped two more streamers and watched as they landed in a clearing to the north of the canyon. He shouted to Jed, showed him the landing zone, and Jed nodded. About a hundred yards from the fire, it felt a little close for comfort, especially with the wind driving against them. But it seemed the cleanest drop spot available.

Jed gave a quick glance at his team—Riley and Hannah appeared a little white-faced. CJ, however, grinned, as did Conner and Pete. Pete reminded him, sometimes, of Kate—

too eager to jump, to fly into the flames.

Tucker, for all his bravado, seemed grim faced.

Jed gave them a thumbs-up, sat down in the door, and waited for the tap. The flames bubbled up below him, and not for the first time he wondered just why he thought it might be a good idea to jump into what seemed like a boiling cauldron of fire for a living.

He'd had a good job as a crew boss for the Hotshots. Perhaps he'd taken the smokejumping position because he, too, had something to prove. Like today—keeping his crew safe.

Cliff tapped his shoulder and Jed launched. The exhilaration hit him, a gasp, tugging at his breath. Then the jerk, and his chute deployed, filled, and he floated.

The smoke found his nose as he grabbed his toggles, steered clear of the fire, over a stand of towering spruce, and into the open.

He landed hard, rolled, and popped up just in time to see CJ on his tail, landing in a graceful roll, used to hitting the dirt from his bull riding days. Behind him floated Conner, then Riley.

Jed removed his gear, shucked off his jumpsuit, and looked up to see Pete, then Tucker, who overshot the drop, nearly hit a tree, and managed to land dangerously close to the edge of the blaze. He came running, dragging up his chute.

Then Hannah, floating down as if she had wings. Her landing, however, had him wincing, one eye closed, and he met Conner's grimace.

Of course Kate landed with a grace that shamed them all. He radioed up to Gilly and she came around, Cliff dropping out their gear.

The fire packs and five-gallon container of water drifted from the heavens.

Jed spread the map out, gestured his team in. "Once Pete and CJ unpack the cargo, we'll fortify the tail, then spread out along the flanks." In his head, he'd already made a plan, and now distributed the assignments without a glance at Conner. *Let her do her job. Which, by the way, you'll have to start doing if you want to be a leader instead of a lovesick boy.*

"Kate, I need you and Hannah to hustle up along the ridge on lookout. We'll head up the left flank and call in a drop along the riverbed, try and put down the fire along the eastern flank."

He expected an argument, even a rolling of the eyes at his decision to send Kate into the safer area, but she simply began stepping out of her jumpsuit, arranging her personal gear bag. He handed her a radio. "Conner and I will stay here at the tail, make sure it stays tamed, and see if we can get his toy working. Keep a weather eye on the fire and call in any wind shifts."

For the first time since she'd arrived, Kate met his eyes. "No problem, Boss."

No problem?

"Be careful." He couldn't help it.

She nodded, offered him the barest grin. "Always. C'mon, Hannah."

Always?

He watched her bug out, almost at a jog, her Pulaski over her shoulder, Hannah on her tail.

No, really, be careful. He barely suppressed the urge to run after her.

The rest of their gear had landed around the zone, and he confirmed it on the radio, said good-bye to Gilly. "Stand by for the second crew."

Conner had unpacked his drone, started assembling the

remote airplane, about two feet long with a detachable wing assembly. Jed stood over him. "How does this thing work?"

Conner picked it up, turned it over. "This camera will record the heat index and wind speeds and give us a look at the fire." He pointed to his iPad mini. "It'll display the results here."

Pete appeared, a chainsaw over his shoulder, on his way to the left flank. "Who's my swamper?"

"CJ, Riley, and Tucker will work on the scratch lines. The wind is with us—let's dig out a line and start a burnout to the tail—the black will keep it from blowing back. Conner, get that thing up, and then report what you see. Guys—on me, we need to shore up the tail."

The team dug into the fifty feet of scratch line at the tail, on the far edge of their jump zone. Behind them, the fire snapped and popped, a spruce occasionally torching deep in the body of the fire, black smoke boiling up in an angry black finger. The air simmered with the stench of burning resin.

Conner's drone lifted off over the fire, and Jed couldn't help but watch over Conner's shoulder the close-up, aerial view of the blaze. Mostly black smoke, but Conner's iPad came alive with readings.

Jed lifted his binoculars to see if he could spot Kate on the ridge, but a quick scan revealed nothing.

He didn't want to pray, but the urge welled inside him. Desperation more than faith in God to keep Kate safe.

But he'd sent her clear of the fire, to watch. He'd pay for it later but didn't care.

"Air Attack, this is Ransom. Come in."

"Ransom, this is Air Attack." Neil "Beck" Beckett, piloting the OV-10 Bronco, a guide plane for the Lockheed Hercules 130, their biggest tanker.

"How far out is our load of mud?"

"Standby, Ransom."

Longest ten seconds of his life as he waited. "The fire is in sight. I'll run a practice run, then send the tanker in along the creek bed. We've got three loads—we'll drop them all then send in for more if we need them."

Jed watched as Beck dove in along the canyon, tracing a route for the big tanker.

A few minutes later the C-130 feathered in a load of orange along the eastern flank.

Steam rose to combine with the gray-black clouds.

Beck came back on the line. "It looks like the fire's about a half mile from the river. You might need a couple full loads."

No doubt.

"We'll circle around and give you another drop."

"Roger that."

The plane disappeared in the smoke.

"Burns, Ransom." Kate's voice over the walkie.

"Ransom, Burns. Go ahead."

"We're on top of the ridge, about a half mile from the head. Flame lengths are about thirty feet, and the fire's eating away toward the river. But the wind is shifting, Jed. I can feel the air tremble. My gut is that the head is about to blow up."

"Get higher," he said to Conner. "See if you can give me a decent picture." He peered at the screen as the drone rose, but smoke obscured the view.

Conner pointed to the wind chart. "Like Gilly said, it's making its own weather. The wind is shifting."

Jed toggled the radio. "Can you head back, Kate?"

"I think that's a negative. The fire is climbing up the ridge. But it's slow—and if we can get a tanker in here, it'll put down."

No panic in her voice, but he stepped back, lifted his binoculars again, scanned the ridge. "Get out your mirror—I want to see where you are."

"Roger that."

To the east, the tanker sprayed another load along the smoking fire.

"Pete, I hope you're down there, reinforcing that drop."

"Roger that, Boss," Pete said. "She's whimpering, but we're on it."

Jed was still scanning the horizon with his glass. There—a wink of light, and he found her.

"Got you, Kate." But before she could answer, smoke obscured his vision.

And then he felt it.

As if a hand rolled in, taking the form of a cloud, shifting the air around him. In a breath that scattered embers and flame into the black around him, it swept across the canyon from the east, picking up speed, curling in a wave up the ridge.

Driving the fire right toward Kate.

"Kate! Get out of there! The wind has shifted. The fire is headed right for you."

Silence.

"Kate?"

"Roger that. We're heading over the ridge and down to the river."

Yes. Good thinking, Kate.

He searched for them again, then turned to Conner. "Find them."

CHAPTER 10

N O NEED TO SCARE Hannah.

Or herself.

Because Kate could handle this. She'd been following her instincts for the past twenty minutes, across the ridge, an eye on the fire, calculating the distance to the river below, keeping her voice low and calm as embers shot over their heads from the flames chewing up the ridge some two hundred yards below.

They had plenty of time before the fire roared up the ridge.

However, the safety of the river seemed ominously far away. She'd felt it in her gut, the hunger of the fire as she'd climbed the backside of the ridge. With the dark, brooding thunderclouds overhead, she recognized fire weather in the making, the kind that created a storm, sent a blaze flooding through a forest at a mile a minute.

But she hadn't wanted to panic Jed—and why, really, when she could be wrong.

Or, not.

At least she'd made the right decision to hike to the apex of the ridge, or they would have been caught scrambling up-hill. Now, all they had to do was find a path down the opposite side, take refuge in the river below.

Kate broke into a jog. "We'll be fine," she said, glancing behind her to Hannah, who kept up, her face pinched, her skin dark with sweat and smoke. She'd said nothing since Kate's last dispatch to Jed.

Kate toggled her radio. "Burns, Ransom. When that tanker gets here, we could use a drop on this side of the canyon, just for safe measure."

Black smoke roiled up behind them, and her eyes burned, her nose thick under her bandanna, now pulled up.

"We're not going to make it!" Hannah's voice, for the first time edged with fear. Kate turned, her gaze fierce. "Yes, we are."

But, below them, the fire had grown, pushed by the wind. Embers crackled over their heads, a ball of fire landed just a hundred feet away, exploding a juniper. Hannah's eyes widened, but she managed not to scream. Cinders landed on her shoulders, and Kate brushed them off Hannah. "We're going to be fine."

She turned, her heart clogging her throat as she started into a jog. "Status on that tanker, Jed?"

Static. She called again, but he didn't answer. Fire weather. Or simply mountain, obscured their signal.

Hopefully—please no—he hadn't done something stupid and come up here looking for her.

Her boots slipped on the narrow hiking path—a mere hopscotch for the fire at this rate.

An explosion ripped through the air and she turned to see the fire crowning, torching treetops as it raced along the canyon. Spot fires ignited pockets of brush and juniper. The blaze crawled up the ridge.

Kate tucked the radio into her pants pocket and took off

in a run along the top, jumping boulders, following the trail toward a tourist lookout. Sweat beaded down her face and shirt, her breaths coming in gulps—and behind her, Hannah struggled, her breath labored. Smoke settled over the top of the ridge, fogged them in, blinding her.

Kate missed the edge of the cliff and nearly launched herself into space. If not for Hannah, she would have crashed over, right down the rocky face that cascaded to the river.

Instead, Hannah lunged for her, grabbing her shirt, jerking her back. Kate slammed against the edge of the embankment, scrubbing her bottom against the rocks and brush, kicking out boulders as she fought for purchase, her breath coming hard. "Whoa—!"

A half mile below, at the bottom of a tumble of Volkswagen-sized boulders, black spruce, and cut, gleaming ledgerock, snaked a glistening ripple of river, the enticing safety of crystalline blue water.

The fire hadn't reached it yet. But the flames raced along the canyon floor.

"We can't make it," Hannah said in a choked whisper.

"No." Kate scrambled back to the trail, calculating the speed of the fire below, the threat behind them, and, on the other side of the ridge, the sheer-face cliff which made this trail so spectacular on a clear, sunny day.

She schooled her voice. "Jed, if you can hear me, we're trapped. We need a drop right at the top of the ridge." She met Hannah's eyes, her jaw tight, then glanced behind her, at the fire. A trickle of flames had burned across the top, met the scrub trail, and looked like they might be dying, but from below, the fire charged up the ridge, consuming the scraggly spruce that grew at an angle.

If she had a chute, she might just leap off the edge, take her chances in the sky.

She nearly jumped at Jed's voice, crackling through the line. "Five minutes out, Kate. Conner's trying to locate you. Where are you?"

Conner? He wasn't coming up the mountain—"Turn him around, Jed. No one is getting through—"

"He's got his drone. Give us your position."

A rush of relief, but even a drone hadn't a hope of finding them in this cloud of smoke.

"I'm on the ridge—Jed, it's getting pretty hot up here."

Hannah had dropped her Pulaski, and Kate indicated for her to pick it up.

More crackling over the radio, his voice choppy.

"Jed?"

Static.

Kate slipped the radio into her leg pocket. Through the blackened smoke, she glimpsed tongues of fire consuming a nearby baby pine, just forty yards below. She met Hannah's wide, stricken eyes. "Do you trust me?"

Hannah nodded.

Kate grabbed her hand. "Follow me." Then she ran, full out, back into the smoke, dragging Hannah behind her. "The only safe place is in the black!"

She kicked away the flames, dodging the embers as the brush burned around her. Below her, the flame lengths reached fifty feet high, arching toward her, jumping from tree to tree.

Embers rained down, hitting her helmet, the collar of her shirt, and she slapped at them, her eyes tearing, the smoke choking her. The flames behind them had quieted, having consumed the fuel and dying at the edge of the trail. If she could find some cool black...she'd spotted a dip in the ridge on her flight to the top, had lodged it in her brain, and now she calculated the distance.

Behind her, Hannah was crying, coughing. Flames flickered at Kate's ankles, her feet crunching through a thin layer of ash. Bits of charred aspen leaves, pine cones, and needles rode the gusts that cycloned from below, incendiaries that singed their shirts, their bandannas.

"Here—we're here!" Kate nearly fell to her knees as the ground dipped below them, a roughened patch of trail washed out by some tributary, scarred, burned over in a light, rippled layer of a flash blaze. It created a clear cut across the trail about five feet wide, just as deep.

Around them, fire crackled in the thicker tundra, pulsing, alive.

But the dirt in the wash was dry, bare.

Kate gripped her Pulaski and swung it down. "Dig yourself a hole!" She scraped at the ground, digging out a hole to breathe, to pocket herself in. "The fire's going to jump the ridge!"

Beside her, Hannah scrabbled at the ground, digging a well into the rocks. The wind snarled, ferocious as it swirled around them. Smoke hung in the air, black and thick. The fire inside it crackled.

"Deploy your fire shelter!"

Hannah dropped her Pulaski and stared at Kate.

"Now, Hannah." Kate grabbed her fire shelter as Hannah fumbled with hers. Around them, the flames leaped three stories high, raining down fire.

Not again. Please.

The wind ripped the shelter from Hannah's hands, and Kate reached out and caught it—reflex more than training.

She shoved the shelter back at Hannah, who gripped the

edges, shaking.

"C'mon. Just like we practiced—feet in the bottom, drop, and pull it over you."

Hannah shoved her feet in the bottom pockets, grabbed the top edge, and pulled the silver Kevlar over her shoulders, falling face down in the dirt.

Kate grabbed her own shelter, the heat scorching her face.

"Stick your face into that hole and breathe the cool air!" She fell, face down into the dirt, anchoring the edges with her feet, her gloved hands. "Don't leave your shelter!"

Please. They wouldn't get the brunt of the blaze, and with the lack of fuels, the radial heat might not be enough to melt the shelter. But with the fire cresting over them, the shelter could supercharge with heat—and her biggest struggle would be convincing Hannah not to lose it, run out into hell. "It's going to be okay!"

Kate anchored the tent with her elbows, her hands, and leaned her forehead on her helmet, sunk her face into the dirt.

The hole still secured the cool breath of humidity despite the flashover—she'd dug deep enough to protect her lungs.

"Ransom, Burns. Come in."

Her radio buzzed in her pocket. Outside, the fire thundered, angry, the shelter swelling with heat. Sweat rolled down her face, drenched her body. Outside, the world glowed red through the pinpricks of light into the shelter.

It wouldn't be long now.

Seconds. She grabbed her radio, dropped it beside her mouth.

"Jed...It's Kate. We're on top of the ridge. We had to deploy. We need..." She took a breath, wincing.

Help. We need help.

Next to her, Hannah started whimpering. "I don't want to die—I don't want to die—"

"Hannah. Shh. Stay in your shelter. We're going to live through this—just stay calm."

She put her elbow in the pocket, kept her hand on the walkie. Her arm sizzled in contact with the fabric of the shelter, and she bit down on her lip to keep from crying out.

"Kate, come in! Answer me!"

Outside, the roaring climaxed as the dragon consumed the forest, rising above the ridge. The breath lifted the edges of her shelter, and embers scooted in, burning through her pants.

She bit her lip but couldn't deny a whimper.

Then, because she didn't know what else to do, because she couldn't think, couldn't believe—— "Jed. I'm scared. I'm really scared. Please...help me."

She wasn't sure if he'd heard her, could never know, because the fire crowned, and in a roar, the demon's hand washed over her.

Next to her, Hannah screamed.

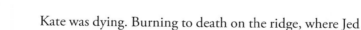

Kate was dying. Burning to death on the ridge, where Jed had sent her to keep her safe.

Jed pressed the walkie to his forehead, sweat dripping down his back, shaking. He toggled the com again. "Kate!"

Static on her end.

Even from here, the heat seared his skin, the smoke tearing his eyes, scorching his lungs as the fire blew up, charging up the ridge, torching spruce in plumes of angry flames that scorched the sky. Smoke clogged the canyon, rolling out in a wave of acrid death, and the air shook, the rumble of a locomotive low and menacing.

I'm scared. At least he thought those might've been her words—they'd cut in and out, choppy, broken.

Not unlike his breath, the beating of his heart.

He put his binoculars to his eyes, scanned the ridge, but the smoke boiled up, over the top, obscuring all hope of spotting them. "Conner, find them!"

Conner had dropped to his knees, scanning his iPad, the drone high above the treetops, dodging torches of black spruce and lodgepole pine. "I have no reference point."

"Air Attack, can you get me a visual on my jumpers? They're in shelters on the western ridge." He fought the panic from his voice. "And I need an ETA on that drop—"

"Smoke's too heavy on the ridge, we can't get close enough for a visual or a drop. Air Attack is circling, trying to locate your jumpers."

"We need a drop over the ridge line, now."

"We only have one load left—if we drop in the wrong location—"

The deep thrumming of the C-130 vibrated above the valley, too high for the retardant to save them.

"Kate, you still with me?" Jed had abandoned any formality, closed his eyes, as he willed for her voice to come crackling through the line.

More static, and he realized he was holding his breath.

Behind him, his crew had widened the line, and he'd already called in the second load of jumpers from Gilly, although with the cyclone of air over the canyon, they'd have to drop from higher, farther out, the fire too dangerous for a closer deployment.

The rest of his team, along the eastern edge of the canyon, had taken advantage of the wind shift to fortify the line, their job now to watch for slop-over and spot fires.

But he knew that every eye was trained on the ridge, dread rising as they watched Kate and Hannah fight for their lives.

"I think I found 'em," Conner said, and Jed dropped to his knees beside him. The drone hovered above the ridge, and Conner held it steady as he pointed on the screen to a shiny blip in the fabric of the smoke and blaze. Two tiny shelters resembling sleeping bags tucked in a niche, fire and smoke licking over the tops as the fire leaped the apex of the ridge and rained down the far side.

It had to be over a hundred degrees in those fire domes.

"Smart. Going into the black, finding that niche. If they sit tight, the blaze will arch right over them," Conner said.

Jed studied the screen for signs of life. Nothing, except for the fact that the shelters' edges didn't fly up with the torrent of wind and ash, evidence that Hannah and Kate fought to keep them pinned.

Smart, indeed. In the pocket of dirt, they might find protection even from the wind and arching of the blaze as it licked over the top of the ridge. Still, flame lengths of fifty feet torched off nearby pines, the entire ridge alight with fire and ash.

Kate and Hannah might suffocate before they burned.

He put a hand to his chest, his knees weak.

"Can you get those images to Air Attack?" Jed said. "We need a load of retardant on their position right now."

"No. But I'll see if I can figure out a reference point." Conner piloted the drone higher, staring at the screen, and Jed moved away, sat on the ground, his gaze through his binoculars to the last place he'd spotted her.

Help me.

He put his walkie to his lips. "Kate," he said softly, eyes on the shelter. "I don't know if you can hear me, but if you can, hang on. Just...hang on. I've ordered a retardant, and they're trying to find you."

He closed his eyes, his memory bringing to him the feel of her body trembling as she pressed against him in the heat of their shelter. "If I could, I'd be there with you right now. Better, I'd take your place." He cut his voice to a whisper. "But I know I can't always be there to protect you, no matter how much I want to. Nor do you need me to. But...I'm scared too, Kate. Because I got you into this, and if anything happens to you..." His throat clogged, and he bent his head into his arms, shaking.

Please, God. We need help.

He didn't know where the prayer came from, maybe an errant thought from so many years ago, a splinter of memory, spoken in her voice—or maybe his. But he let the prayer linger, solidify.

We need help.

He lifted his gaze to the ridge, a flame, hot and lethal, and heard her last words in the walkie, a fist in his soul.

Help me.

Yes. He took a breath, and because he didn't know the words, he began to hum.

CHAPTER 11

IF KATE DIDN'T KEEP Hannah calm, the girl might end up swallowing a lungful of toxic, deadly fumes.

But in the shelter next to her, Hannah had stopped screaming, started begging, and Kate recognized the signs of someone unraveling.

"Stay in your shelter!"

"It's too hot. I can't—I can't do this!" Hannah's voice shook over the growl of the fire, strumming deep into Kate's bones.

"If you go out there, you might not burn to death, but the super-charged thermal plumes will fry your lungs." She kept her mouth cupped into the dirt. "Stay in your shelter, Hannah. Trust me!"

Judging by the cyclone of wind tugging at her shelter and the flickering glow of flame turning the fabric into pinpricks of orange, they still had a long fight ahead.

Fear had long left her, pooled in her gut, replaced by a searing, dark agony.

She imagined Jed from his position in the canyon below, watching her, his nightmares realized. Tears ran down her nose, dropped into the dirt.

I'm just holding onto the wild, desperate—yeah, okay,

faith—that you won't get hurt. That you'll be smart out there, and that by some grace that I don't deserve, you'll come back to me.

Please, she wanted to come back to him.

Because she *did* love him—much more than fire, more than proving herself, more than the fear that someday she'd show up and he'd have his bags packed.

She closed her eyes, breathed through the sickly sweet, acrid redolence of the fire embedded in her bandanna. The outside world had vanished, only teeth-gritted survival as she zeroed in on enduring. Even Jed, through the coms, died, leaving only static.

Alone.

She shuddered, the heat baking her skin, her hands on fire as she fought the hungry winds ripping at the edges.

Abandoned.

Of course.

But God is for *you, Kate. He is on your side.*

Gilly's voice in her head. Kate's body trembled, sobs now finding her throat, racking up through her chest. *I want to believe that, God. I really want to believe that, but—*

The static broke through, cracking, broken. She laid her head against the com, longing for his voice. "Jed?"

Not Jed. Or maybe...But she thought she heard humming.

She pressed her ear against the speaker, listening. She knew this song—their song. The one she'd sung to him as he'd shivered, shock overtaking his body, as she'd prayed for him to live.

Great is Thy faithfulness, Oh God my Father...

Jed. Humming to her, the only song he knew that might

give her hope.

Jed...a man without faith singing a song of faith for her.

She sang the words in her soul. *There is no shadow of turning with Thee...*

No shadow of turning...or running.

No, in fact, she'd been the one who had done the running. No wonder she felt alone—God hadn't left her—she'd left *Him.*

And yet He kept showing up, saving her every time she found herself trapped. Giving her a chance to reach out. Ask for help.

Believe in second chances.

Thou changest not, Thy compassions, they fail not.

Oh, she needed that. Because a girl who had flirted with fire as much as she did needed all the endless compassion God would give.

All the protection she could get.

Even in the form of Jed. He'd been there, offering his protection—maybe even God's protection—since the moment she'd decided she wanted to live an over-the-edge crazy, dangerous life.

And for the record—I could probably come to accept you fighting fire if I knew you could see that you had a very good reason to stay alive.

"I do have a good reason to stay alive." Tears blurred her eyes, but she'd been crying for so long from smoke and fumes, it didn't matter. "Jed," she whispered. "I choose you. I want you." *Please God, don't let it be too late.*

Outside, the cyclone hummed, moaned, and then, with a terrific crack, she heard the thunder of a giant pine crash down, splintering in waves so close to her fire dome the embers bit at it. Shaggy, burning tree limbs brushed the fabric, the heat suddenly soaring.

Beside her, Hannah again began to scream, hysterical.

Oh, God, save us. Kate buried her head in the ground, holding on as her shelter began to crinkle and burn.

I choose you. For a second, Kate's voice crackled through the radio, broken. *I want you.*

Then the radio went silent again. "Kate!" He was on his feet, pacing, calling her name, holding the walkie against his forehead. "Conner, how are you doing on that location?"

"Working on—"

Crackling, then Kate's voice again. "Jed! Help us! We're burning!"

"Kate!" He put the binoculars to his eyes, and his breath stalled as he located a wall of flame, tree fallen, its crown blazing over the well in which they lay.

"Air Attack—we need that drop, right now!"

Nothing on the other end.

Jed leaned over, couldn't breathe.

Then he grabbed a water pump. Strapped it on. Grabbed his Pulaski.

"You can't go, Jed." Conner, on his feet now, grabbed his shirt. "There's nothing you can do—"

"I can't just stay here and watch—listen to her burn to death!" He shook off Conner. "I'm going—"

"And you'll end up dead, just like Jock. And if Kate lives through this, she'll have two men dead by fire, going against their gut to save someone they love."

But wasn't that the point? Having someone to love—and

not being willing to let them go? He shoved Conner away. "I should have never let her walk away in the first place. She needs me."

"I'm sorry, buddy, but—" Conner tackled Jed into the dirt, pinning him, face down. "You're not going."

"Jed!" Screams through the walkie. Jed swung at Conner, pushing him off, but Conner had him in some sort of Green Beret grip, choking him against his arm.

"Let me go!" He elbowed Conner in the gut, heard him grunt, but Conner held on, tenacious.

He was losing this fight—and not because of Conner, but because Conner was right—he'd only arrive in time to discover her smoking corpse.

Not this way. *Oh, God, please, not this way.* He closed his eyes, put his head against the ground. His desperation emerged in a strangled whisper. "Please, God. Help us..."

Conner let him go, standing over him, breathing hard.

Then, crackling, a voice.

"Air Attack, to Ransom. We've just sighted a plume of crowning from the ridge. It seems the fire's jumping the ridge at that point—we're going to drop there, see if we can slow it down."

Jed scrambled for the radio, but Conner got to it first.

"That's them! Drop the retardant! Now!"

Jed launched to his feet, grabbing the radio back from Conner as the deep, heart-rumbling hum of the approaching tanker signaled the beginning of its drop run.

"Hang on, Kate. The drop is on its way."

Nothing on the other end.

The silver bird dropped from the smoky clouds, then, as if it might be bleeding, the plane opened the chute and the retardant sprayed out over the ridge, falling, splattering the fire with muddy reside.

A cough of smoke and the fire gasped, drew back, as if stunned.

"Call in another load," Jed said.

"Another tanker is on the way," Beck confirmed.

"Kate?"

Nothing. As Jed listened, he met Conner's eyes, his jaw tight.

Conner picked up his water pump, his Pulaski.

"What are you doing?"

"I crashed the drone."

"Ransom, this is Gilly. We just dropped the second crew. They should be at your position shortly."

Not soon enough. But moments later, he heard Reuben's voice calling to him through the green. The man appeared at a near run, ready to fight fire, followed by Ned and the rest of the recruits.

Reuben's face looked grim. "Have you heard from them?"

Apparently, they'd been following the transmissions on their coms.

Jed scoured the ridge with his glasses, gauging the color of the smoke. Not quite white, but not the cauldron of black it had been. He almost didn't have the energy to hope, but lifted his walkie anyway. Toggled the switch. "Kate? Come in, Kate."

"C'mon, Boss," Reuben said, motioning to the rookies to follow. "Let's find our teammates."

Jed had already asked God for a favor today, but he lifted another prayer anyway—*Please, God, let her be alive.*

CHAPTER 12

"**K**ATE—ARE YOU STILL THERE?"

Hannah's voice whispered across the crackling of the gasping embers, under the coating of thick ruddy mud, raspy, wavering, as if just barely hiccupping back a fresh onslaught of panic.

Kate lifted her mouth from the burrow where she lay, trembling, bruised, still dizzy from the bath of retardant that slammed down over their enclave. Saving their lives.

Now, the fire crackled and hissed around them, a dragon, gulping for life, dying.

"I'm here, Hannah. We're okay."

"I'm burned. The fire came through my shelter, burned my legs."

Kate felt pretty sure her elbows were singed, but her adrenaline kept her from feeling it. "We're going to be fine, Hannah. We just have to wait—the air is still toxic."

And, in reality, she didn't know exactly how they might extricate themselves. Her shelter seemed pinned to the ground, shaggy limbs pressing against the fabric under a coating of slime that turned the world to shadow.

Her best guess—a snag had fallen over their hideout.

"They'll never find us—we're buried here, and besides,

you don't know that they're okay. Jed might have gotten caught in the flames too."

Kate hadn't thought of that in the radio silence, that the fire might have turned— She reached for the radio. "Jed? Are you out there?"

Beside her, Hannah began to sob. "I'm so stupid. I thought I could do this. My dad always teased me about being a smokejumper. But I thought I could do this." More hiccupped sobs. "I had no idea."

No one ever did. "Smokejumping is twenty seconds of exhilaration followed by days of back breaking, chain-gang hard labor. And it isn't for the weak. But—but you've got it, Hannah. We lived, and that counts, and if you want to walk away, you have that knowledge—you faced it, and lived."

More tears, shuddered breath. Around them, the snap and crackle of embers, the rustle of wind.

"You don't think—it won't re-light, will it?"

Kate took a breath, cradling the dead walkie against her ear. "I don't know. But that's why we need to stay put—"

"I'm not staying here!" Groaning—

"Hannah! Don't move. I know it's easier to run. Believe me—I get it. You're hurt and scared and all you think is you have to get out. I get it better than you could ever know—but you can't. Breathe. You'll only make it worse by running."

Only make it worse.

She closed her eyes. She thought she'd been doing them a favor by walking out of their lives, pushing them to the perimeter of her life. But she'd only made it worse—for all of them.

I'm sorry, Dad. I'm so sorry.

Jed was right—there was no room for him when she belonged to fire. But maybe God had given her a way out when

He'd saved her, not once, but now three times. And maybe her legacy wasn't being the strongest, the bravest, but, like Jed said—building the family her father had longed for.

With Jed, her father's favorite hotshot.

Her eyes closed, and for the first time—probably in three years— the buzz of fear always under her skin, in the back of her mind and low in her gut, vanished.

She didn't have to be Blazin' Kate Burns if she didn't want to be.

Next to her, Kate heard fabric tearing, then a gasp as Hannah broke free of her shelter.

"Hannah!" Kate lifted the edge of her own shelter, got a swift and brutal look at their situation. The tree had indeed fallen, not quite on them, but nearby. The burning branches had arched over them, the pocket of earth protecting them from being crushed.

Hannah was on her knees chopping at the tree with her Pulaski, crying. Cinders and ash rained down over her, singeing her shirt, stirring oxygen into the trunk, swirling the flames to life.

In her panic, she might just ignite a cauldron of fire right here in their nook.

In a second, Kate rose to her knees, pushed back the shelter and grabbed Hannah. Kate wound her hand around Hannah's waist, jerked her to herself, and threw her on the ground. Hannah struggled beneath her, but Kate pressed herself over her, her hand over her arm. "Still! Lie still!"

Then she hooked her legs around Hannah and grabbed for the edges of the shelter, pulling it back up.

Hannah struggled under her, nearly hysterical.

"Breathe, Hannah. Just breathe." Hannah had lost her helmet, and Kate covered her head with her own. "Listen to me. The worst is over. We lived—and we're going to keep on living as long as you keep calm. But you have to work with me. We're going to lie here and wait."

Hannah trembled, shaking her head, still fighting her. "They're not coming! No one is coming—they're all dead!"

Hannah's words had the power to scrape Kate raw, but she swallowed it all down, found her voice, and in it heard the faintest hue of her father. "Listen, Hannah. Whatever happens, we're going to remember that we are not alone. Never alone. You have me, and I have you, and..." She closed her eyes, and a voice bubbled up, something strong and solid.

The voice she'd come back to Montana to find.

"We have God." She leaned into the memory, could nearly feel her father's hand on her cheek, his voice in her ear.

"When I was a little girl, my dad would leave, sometimes for weeks on end to fight fire. He'd leave me with Gilly's family's, so I was safe, but I was still always so terrified—I admit it—that he'd never come back. But I was too proud to tell him. I didn't want him to think I was weak. He still knew. I *know* he knew, because he would always say the same thing. We'd pray the same four verses together every time he had to leave."

She took a breath. "Teach me your way, Lord, that I may rely on your faithfulness; give me an undivided heart, that I may fear your name. I will praise you, Lord my God, with all my heart; I will glorify your name forever."

She could hear him then, the soft, resonant tenor, the smell of him, pine, wood smoke, sometimes the slick scent of his Brut aftershave. His big hand, smoothing back her hair, the color of his own. Green eyes holding hers. "For great is your love toward me; you have delivered me from the depths, from the realm of the dead."

Tears welled in her eyes. "Give me a sign of your goodness, that my enemies may see it and be put to shame, for you, Lord, have helped me and comforted me."

His kiss, pressed to her cheek. *Do not be afraid, Katie. God is with me.*

I'm not trying to break your heart here, but what if you had stuck around, let your dad teach you his tricks?

But he had passed along his tricks—all of them, from his firefighting knowledge to his unquenchable dedication to his team, to the one thing she really needed—

Faith. And yes, she might have walked away from it, but there it was, embedded inside her.

And it was embedded in his protégé, Jed, too.

"Don't worry, Hannah. Help is on the way. Because if there is one thing I know about Jed, it's that he will not give up on us. It's his most annoying, wonderful trait." She grabbed at the edge of the shelter as the wind tried to whip it up. "Even if it takes his last breath, he'll find us, I guarantee it."

"How can you be so sure?"

Even as she said it, the wind began to stir the shelter, the air pocket gathering heat. No, please. Not again.

But she kept her voice calm, held onto Hannah. "Because it's something he learned from my father, the indomitable Jock Burns."

If they didn't move faster, Jed might lose his mind. But he'd already fallen twice as he fought his way up the devastated hiking trail, his footing slick against the slurry-soaked rocks, the spongy, ashy burnout. Retardant coated the scrub trees, the grasses, all the way to the balding, charred top of the ridge.

His smokejumpers scrambled up behind him along the smoky, snap-crackle-and-popping edge of the fire, dousing it as they went with their water canisters, hoping that the wind didn't decide to betray them.

The fire continued to rage along the canyon, but with another drop of retardant along the opposite side, the blaze would die at the river.

Still no word from Kate on the radio.

Twenty feet from the top of the ridge, nearly two hundred yards ahead, Jed spotted the carcass of a once-towering black spruce toppled over the groove where he hoped Kate lay in her shelter. "Kate!"

With the crackling of smoke and fire, the wind carried his voice downhill.

"Hey, Boss!" Reuben's voice turned him, and his breath caught on the site of a destroyed, blackened shelter, held in Reuben's gloved hand. "I found it lying against a snag."

Below him, he heard Conner stifle a word.

No! Jed scrabbled up the ridge, nearly on his hands and knees. "Reuben, get that saw up here!"

Jed slipped, slammed his knee against a rock, but found his footing and hit the ridge at a run.

The tree lay blackened, still sizzling, refusing to die under the bloody wash of retardant. It hadn't fallen directly on the hole; instead it lay just along the lip, the bushy arms arching over the top, as if protecting it from the sparks and embers, the heavy blaze of a rolling fire.

In a way, the tree had acted as a barrier to the greater fireball. He grabbed at the branches, chopped them away, the trunk barring him from climbing over, or under, moving around it. But, he could plainly see the other shelter, crumbled, burned, but intact.

And unmoving.

"Kate! We're here!" He motioned to Reuben as he laid into the tree with his Pulaski. Branches broke, but not enough for him to launch himself through its bushy grasp.

"Step back, Boss!" Reuben fired up his chainsaw with a growl, and Jed fell back long enough for Rube to divide the trunk in two pieces—then more. Jed didn't wait as he threw them out of the way and used his Pulaski to push through the final, charred branches.

He leaped down into the enclave.

Oh—his breath wavered, his hands shaking as he reached out to the shelter. *Please—*

He peeled it back.

Kate lay halfway on Hannah, her legs locked around her, arm against her neck, her face turned to the ground. Hannah lay beneath her, her trousers charred, her shirt pocked with cinder burns.

"Kate!

Then, as his breath caught, she lifted her head. Eyes watering, her bandanna pulled up over her nose, blackened with smoke, she stared at him.

He was in the hole in a second, reaching for her.

She pushed herself up, her hands shaking. "You—you came. You're—"

"Here." He caught her hand. "I'm here."

His knees threatened to buckle as he reached for her, trying not to cry. "I thought you were dead." Even as he said it, he scanned her body. She looked intact, if not grimy, her face streaked with dirt and soot.

"I'm okay. I think I'm okay—"

But he couldn't wait. Just grabbed her up, pulling her to

himself, holding on.

His entire body shook, and she crumpled against him, her head buried in his chest.

Shuddering.

And then, because he couldn't stay in this grave for a second longer, he picked her up in his arms, dropping his Pulaski and carrying her out of the hole. Out of the corner of his eye, he saw Conner drop in behind him to attend to Hannah.

And then, it was all Kate as he set her on the ground on the blackened ridge top. He knelt next to her, whipping his bandanna from his neck, wiping her face, her neck. "I tried to call you—"

"I heard you." She pulled off her gloves, reached up to touch his cheek. "You hummed a song to me."

"I did more than that, Kate." He pressed his forehead to hers. "I prayed. I begged. I had nothing but hope and—"

"The tree. It came down, and then the retardant followed." She nodded, as if piecing it together. "They couldn't find us, could they?"

"No. The smoke blackened the entire ridge."

"And the tree—they followed the flames."

He nodded. Swallowed. "I...when I saw that ridge go up, I thought—oh, Kate." Yep, he was going to be sick. He turned away, leaned his head to the ground, fighting the urge.

She was beside him, her hand on his back. "I lived—we lived. Shh."

He managed to pull it together without making a fool of himself—although maybe he was long past that—and turned back to her, his heart still a fist pounding his chest.

She stood there, grime on her face, her eyes bloodshot, her nose runny, her hair in sweaty tangles, and he knew he'd never seen anyone more beautiful. "You. Are, Brilliant."

"Huh?"

"The crevice—that was brilliant." He cradled her face in his hands. "You're brilliant. And terrifying. And I'm so in love with you I don't care. I want it all."

Because, yeah, it hit him. That was exactly his Kate. Brilliant. Terrifying. And that made him stretch out his hand to something that might keep him sane—faith. Clearly God loved her, because really, she had a crazy kind of luck.

The kind of crazy—divine—luck that a guy needed if he were to love her. "I love you so much, it consumes me, and I go a little crazy with it, but—it also makes me want to be the guy who shows up in your life, with a Pulaski and, yeah, maybe a prayer. Because loving you requires me to have faith, and that's a good thing."

She smiled then, soft, long. "Really?"

"That, or I'll slowly lose my mind." He lifted a shoulder.

And right there, in front of the entire team now putting out spot fires and sawing apart the snag, she kissed him. Curled her hand around his neck and pulled his mouth to hers in a kiss that could probably leave blisters.

She smelled of smoke, tasted of sweat, and trembled a little with the lingering fear of the fire, but, as he wrapped his arms around her, he heard her words.

I want you, Jed.

Him. Not fire.

And in his arms, her kiss turned unexpectedly ardent, the residue, perhaps, of too much adrenaline.

Not that he minded. So he pulled her close but slowed them down because, yeah, they had a fire to put out. Or at least bank.

Especially with Reuben, Conner, and the rest of his team looking on.

But really, he didn't care. Because that's how it was to love Blazin' Kate Burns. Risk, not recklessness. And, hand-in-hand, jumping with a cry of faith straight into the fire.

EPILOGUE

*A*RE YOU SURE THIS *is what you want?*

Miles's voice echoed in Kate's head as she sat at her picnic table overlooking the base. The Twin Otter airplane with its red stripes gleamed under the early morning sun, now gilding the tarmac with gold and the red-flamed hues of morning.

Cars had started to arrive on base, hotshots reporting for roll call, even on a Sunday during fire season.

She wouldn't be reporting. Not anymore. *Yes, this is what I want.*

Telling Jed, however—she didn't exactly know how to approach that.

She took another sip of coffee, only slightly wincing at the pull of new skin still healing on her forearms. Second degree burns—not enough for grafts, but it had sidelined her long enough to get her head around the fire, the churning emotions.

The idea that she had a choice.

Overhead the sky appeared cloudless, but the hint of heat slithered in with the morning air, slipping down into the valley of Ember with the scent of pine and aspen.

Across the way, Jed's house sat dark—she guessed he must still be deployed on a booster trip to help with mop-up on a fire south of Spokane. He'd called from his spike camp, finding a rare pocket of reception, and it unnerved her how she leaned into his voice, the sweet baritone of it sliding under her skin to linger even after the call.

Yes, this might be the bravest thing she'd ever done.

The sound of the motor, thundering up behind the camper, made her turn, and by the time she'd swung her leg over the bench and gotten up, Jed had parked and was heading up her walk.

She met him at the edge of the deck.

The sight of Jed Ransom, striding toward her with a smile, eagerness in his eyes, never failed to spark heat inside her, and now the sense that this amazing man, all six-foot-two of him, with his wide shoulders, muscled arms, the overwhelming power of his love, belonged to her—

Maybe it didn't take as much courage as she thought.

He wore a pair of jeans, a blue T-shirt, and his flip-flops, his dark hair glistening from a recent shower. He hadn't shaved, however—five days of growth on his chin showed flecks of gold and copper. And he smelled—well, not quite like he might be on fire, but the smoky scent still embedded his skin, mingling with the lathering of soap.

But his gaze fell on her and, yes, where there was smoke...

"Babe," he said simply and caught her up in his arms. She wrapped hers around his neck and melted into his kiss, any lingering fear dissolving in the certainty of his touch.

He set her down on the porch steps, softened his kiss, then cupped her face in his hands, meeting her eyes, smiling. His thumbs caressed her cheek, leaving little eddies of tingle all the way through her body. "Ready for breakfast?"

Huh?

He let her go then and turned back to the bike, parked

behind the camper. In a moment, he returned with a container. "Jock and I had a tradition. Every Sunday, if we were home, he'd make us flapjacks."

He opened the container.

A stack of fresh pancakes lay inside, still steaming.

"You cook?" Kate asked.

"One of us has to," he said, winking. "I even brought syrup." He produced a bottle in his other hand.

"Wow," Kate said. She ducked into the camper, grabbing forks and two plates.

Jed was sitting at the table when she returned. He dished her up a stack, she added syrup, and they ate in amiable silence.

"Is this Dad's recipe? Because I taste nutmeg."

Jed nodded.

"You know, it was the only thing he could make, right? We lived on frozen pizza and boxed macaroni and cheese most of the time."

"Sometimes he'd invite the rookies over, feed them flapjacks until they burst," Jed said. "And then he'd invite them to church."

She laughed. "Sounds like Dad."

But Jed's face had sobered. "I was thinking it might be time for me to take him up on that offer."

She put down her fork. Glanced past him, toward town, to the white spire of the Ember Community Church bell tower. "Really?"

"Eat up. Then put something on besides pajamas."

She changed into a clean pair of jeans and a T-shirt that didn't have a logo on it, then tied her hair back, and returned to find Jed standing by his bike, holding a helmet. "I'm driving."

"Of course you are." She got on behind him, wrapping her arms around that tight, washboard waist.

It felt so natural to hold onto him, nudging herself close as they drove down to Ember, motoring along the side streets, past the Hotline, now dark and recuperating, the grocery store—closed on Sundays—the Spotfire Diner, packed with breakfasters. "When did you guys get in?"

"Last night, real late," Jed said. "I was going to come by, but...well, I'm finding it harder to listen to Jock's voice in my head. Trying to be on my best behavior."

She kissed his neck. "You're a good man, Jed Ransom."

His hand went to hers, clasped around his waist, and squeezed.

They pulled up to the church parking lot—packed this Sunday with pickups and 4x4s, although many of the locals simply walked. A hymn peeled out of the windows of the old white building. Wide steps led straight into the sanctuary—around back, they'd added a Sunday school wing and offices.

She scuffed her foot on her initials in the bottom step. He noticed it and smiled. "You can take the lady out of the church, but you can't take the church out of the lady."

Maybe. She hoped so. But she paused as she stood at the entrance.

Her dad's memory permeated this place—sitting next to him in the pew after her mother left was the only solid, sane thing she could hold onto. That and the fire camp. The congregation sat, the hymn finished, and she recognized so many of them, including Gilly and her row of brothers, her sister, still lined up on the left side, near the front.

Jed took her hand, led her into the sanctuary, and she glanced at him.

Since when was he eager to step into the Lord's embrace? Except, maybe he was doing the brave thing, too.

She squeezed his hand as they looked for an open pew, hoping to sneak in as Pastor John Priest—yes, she always laughed at that irony of Gilly's dad being the town clergy— took the pulpit.

But as they headed for a space near the back on the right, she knew it wouldn't work.

A ripple of surprise, turned heads, and then Pastor John blew their cover. "We see you, Kate Burns—and you, too, Jed, trying to sit in the back. But there's a perfectly good space up in front, in the pew your father loved. Where he could hear my sermon and make faces at me when he disagreed."

A ripple of laughter.

Kate had stilled, not looking at Jed. But he shrugged and pulled her up to the front, leading the way into the pew.

"Before you sit, Kate—and Jed—we're so glad you're here. I think we'd all like to thank you for what you did."

What they did? But applause lit up the room, and she stared at the crowd, nonplussed. "I didn't—"

And then she spied Ray and Ellen Butcher heading down the aisle, Gemma Turnquist leading the way. Hannah behind them, her leg still wrapped—her own second-degree burns putting a stall on her smokejumping, for now.

She grinned at Kate, smiled. And, apparently, she'd been talking, because Gemma leaned over the front pew and pulled Kate close. "I'm sorry," she whispered.

Ray clasped Jed's hand, clamped him on the shoulder. Nodded. Then he turned to Kate. "You are your father's daughter," he said and hugged her.

She sat, a little dazed for the rest of the sermon, her hand locked into Jed's.

Her father's daughter.

Yes, she was. She couldn't help a smile. No, this wouldn't take any courage at all.

Jed had sat through the service without once wanting to bolt. Even let the sermon settle into him, his fingers woven into Kate's grip, the sunshine streaming through the arched, stained-glass windows.

This, exactly this, was how he planned on surviving this summer and every one after this. Because it came to him during the last deployment, as he'd sat in strike camp, fighting to get a signal to just hear her voice, that it didn't matter if Kate jumped or not.

She took his heart with her into every decision she made, risky or not. And if he wanted to love her well, he'd have to go all in. Jump into this life beside her, come what may, clinging to her hand and believing...well, believing that God would keep showing up, through every fire, and beyond.

They rose for the final hymn, and he found himself humming along, a familiar song to even him.

Amazing grace! How sweet the sound...

He hadn't thought much about grace, but believing in that, too, was part of the hold on faith. Grace for today, for tomorrow...

"Through many dangers, toils, and snares, I have already come..."

Kate sang beside him as if she'd never missed a Sunday, her voice robust, resonant, and he looked down at her, caught a hint of a smile.

Her eyes were closed, her face raised to the heavens.

I'm trusting her to you, Jed.

The voice shook him, sliding through his bones, wrapping around his chest. Jock. Jed could almost feel the man's presence beside him, his hand heavy on his shoulder. Jed had the crazy urge to look for him and even glanced toward the empty space beside him.

Nothing, of course, but the heat of the sunlight gilding the wooden pew in the stained-glass shades of red, amber, gold. Firelight.

"'Tis grace hath brought me safe thus far, And grace will lead me home."

Yeah, maybe Jock Burns was here, because a curl of warmth—peace, maybe—breathed through Jed.

Kate now opened her eyes, looked up at him, grinning as he sang the final verse.

Maybe God loving him wasn't such a crazy gamble.

They glad-handed their way out of church, ending with John Priest. "For a second, seeing you in Jock's pew, I had a glimpse of him, so many years ago. You do him proud, Jed." He winked then gathered Kate in a hug.

Whispered something in her ear, to which she blushed. Really?

But she wouldn't give it away as she walked over to the bike. "I have to show you something," she said, pulling on her helmet. "Can I drive?"

"If I get to hold on," he said quietly, a little husk to his voice.

She gave him a look, added to the blush, but climbed on and waited for him to sit behind her. He settled his hands on her hips as she pulled out of the parking lot.

With luck, today would be theirs—no fire, no callout, nothing but the blue sky arching overhead, the mountains, glorious and beckoning on the horizon. They'd drink lemonade on the deck, watch the wind stir the stars as twilight dropped around them.

He'd try and decide if it was too soon to ask her to marry him.

She was headed back toward her place, along the fire-base road, but instead of turning left, to the ridge, she kept going, deeper into the land.

Her grandfather's property. Once upon a time, they'd run cattle on the rolling hills. To his knowledge, the land had gone wild, untended since the old man died nearly twenty years ago.

They passed dilapidated fencing, old hay barns, and finally pulled up to the small two-story farm house with a sagging front porch and a large dormer window off the front. White paint peeled in curls from the clapboard siding, and plywood nailed over the windows swelled with rain and weather.

Behind the house, a once-white barn sagged, half the roof fallen in, an old International tractor rusting in the front paddock.

Kate pulled up, cut the motor.

He pulled off his helmet. "What are we doing here?"

She worked her helmet off, shook out her beautiful dark-red hair. "I have something to tell you." She held the bike, and he got off. Then she followed and set her helmet on the seat. Headed for the front porch.

"Kate—that's—well, be careful."

She turned around, grinning. "Seriously?"

He lifted his shoulder in a shrug. "Reflex."

She laughed, shook her head, and picked her way up the stairs to the front door. Then, as he followed—he couldn't help it, really, just in case the floor decided to give way—she dug into her pocket.

Produced a key.

She fitted it into the front door lock. Fiddled with it. "Shoot, it's stuck."

He stepped up. "Let me try." He took the handle, wiggled the key, and slowly turned it, feeling the grooves of the lock until the tumblers clicked into place.

The door swung open.

To his shock, the inside had weathered the years well, the entryway floor layered in dust. Two rooms led off the hall-way—a parlor and a family room. They were still intact despite the wallpaper peeling off in swaths.

A stairway led to the upstairs. "There are two bedrooms upstairs according to the plans," Kate said.

"Plans?"

She turned to him, a shine in her eyes he'd never seen before. "Yeah. Plans. Jock drew them up years ago—long before Mom left. He was going to fix up the place, make it our home."

"But after your mom left..."

"I think he couldn't bear it. So many of his dreams for this place included her, our family." She stepped up to Jed. She put her arms around his waist, looking up to meet his gaze, hers sweet and smoldering. "I want to fix it up, Jed. Build our life here."

Build their life.

His expression must have betrayed his surprise because she grinned, then rose up on her tiptoes and kissed him. Sweetly, her hand on his cheek, lingering.

When she lowered herself, her eyes shone. "There's more, Jed. I went into the office today, and I'm going to work in

Overhead as a fire behavior analyst. I'll still train the teams and jump if it's an emergency, but...well, someone needs to stay home and keep the fires burning."

She winked, but he stilled, her words a fist in his chest. "What? No—Kate. I don't want you to have to choose—I was wrong—"

"No, you were right. Not about making me choose, but helping me realize I had the *right* to choose. The fact is, I didn't let fear keep me from jumping, but—I don't love it. I love jumping, but I don't have to fight fires to do that. Most of all, I'm going to make sure that, for every single jump, you have what you need to stay safe and come home, to me." She smoothed her hands over his chest. "Which, you're going to promise to do, right?"

He caught her face in his hands, met her eyes with his. "With everything inside me."

Somewhere in the middle of the rush of emotion that followed, he heard, in the back of his head, the sound of a phone jangling.

Then his pocket started to buzz.

He was sitting on the inside stairs, Kate tucked into his lap. She made a face. "Are you on call?"

He nodded and worked the phone out of his pocket, opened it. "Jed here."

"It's Reuben, and I'm at the office. You'd better get down here, buddy, because we've got problems."

Kate untangled herself from his embrace, got up. He put Reuben on speaker. "'Sup?"

"Amy Fee is here from Boise, with a report on the Powder Ridge fire."

Kate handed him his helmet, and he led the way out the door, now putting the phone to his ear as she locked up.

"Break it down for me, Rube." He walked over to the bike.

"They found another one of those drones at the fire, and they think it might have been deliberately set."

He swung his leg over the bike and moved it off the stand.

"And, since both those fires happened in our backyard..." Reuben didn't have to finish for Jed to figure it out.

He looked at Kate as he spoke into the phone, his voice grim. "We have an arsonist in Jude County, and they're coming after us."

A NOTE FROM THE AUTHOR

Every once in a while, there's a story that just won't leave you alone. It comes to you, relentlessly, knocking at the door of your heart, refusing to go away, despite you telling it that it's not quite time to open the door yet.

Just wait.

But it keeps knocking until, finally you can't take it. You wrestle out of the tangle of deadlines to find a moment in time...and open the door.

And in walks Jed Ransom. Conner Young. Reuben Marshall. Kate Burns. And Pete Brooks (oh, Pete! Swoon!) Jed Ransom and his smokejumper crew have been aching to tell their story for nearly a decade, when I went to the Missoula Smokejumper training base and Jed started tapping me on the shoulder. It only got worse when he showed up in *Take A Chance On Me*, my Christiansen family #1—as a friend of Darek Christiansen.

And then there was poor Conner, who's been waiting for HIS own story since the *Team Hope* days.

How fun to sit down, finally, and write the story of Jed facing his fears of loving a woman who loves adventure. And Kate, the woman who finally gets the man she's always loved. I wanted to write a trilogy that might showcase the brutally long, heroic events of one fiery summer—not unlike the recent summer fires Montana (and other parts of our country) have experienced. And I wanted to set it against a backdrop of faith—letting my jumpers work out their fear and lies and discover truth as they faced life. I took, as my inspirational theme, the words of the hymn, *Great is Thy Faithfulness*, and wove each verse into the three books, hoping the sense of God's presence during our darkest, scariest moments might be felt by my characters. And…by you, my readers. Because He IS there, behind every blaze, every harrowing accident, every moment when life feels overwhelming.

My deepest gratitude goes to Ellen Tarver, Barbara Curtis, David Warren, Lacy Williams and my amazing masterminds who gave me the courage to push me out of the plane and into indie publishing. You are my team.

I hope you'll continue with Conner Young's story—he's met a charming woman named Liza Beaumont, from Deep Haven, MN, and it's about time he gives his heart away…if he has the courage. Check out his story in *Playing with Fire*, then continue the *Summer of Fire* trilogy with Reuben and Gilly's story in *Burnin' For You*. Just maybe, everyone will end the summer without getting burned.

Or not…

Until we meet again—**Go in Grace!**

Susie May

Montana Fire

Book Two
Playing With Fire

Sneak Peek

THIS WAS NOT HOW Liza Beaumont wanted to die.

Not that anyone ever *wanted* to die, but certainly Liza could think of a dozen or more ways that would be preferable to ending up as an early morning snack for a six-hundred-pound grizzly.

First choice might be tucked into the embrace of Conner Young, their golden years fading into a molten sunset, perhaps drifting off into sleep, to wake up in glory.

There she went again, wishing for things she didn't have. Like bear spray. Or a tranquilizer gun.

Or maybe, even decent cell service here, high up on a remote trail in the middle of the Cabinet Mountains in western Montana.

She glanced down the trail, back up at the bear now rocking back and forth. What had the camp wildlife expert said about bears? Stop, drop and roll—no, no—

Drop. Play *dead*. Except her instincts, frankly, were to scream first, then—well, run.

Of course, that was *always* her instinct.

But this time it felt right, because, really, who had the courage to just lay there while a grizzly sniffed her prone body, ready to take a tasty bite out of her neck. Not when she had heaps more life to live, hopes, dreams...

Only, one of those included a six-foot-two blond smoke-jumper with devastating blue eyes, wide sinewed shoulders and a body honed by the rigors of fighting fire who claimed to love sunrises as much as she did.

But Conner wasn't here, was he? Just her, her sharpened colored graphite pencils and a fresh canvas to paint her artist's view of the sunrise. The perfect place to remind herself—and her fellow camper—that they didn't need men to live happi-ly-ever-after.

Except said camper hadn't been in her bunk this morning in the high school girls' cabin.

Esther, where are you?

Clearly not here, on the overlook.

Liza could hardly believe it when she'd woken this morn-ing to the sight of Esther's rumpled, empty sleeping bag. She'd torn herself out of bed, grabbed coffee from the lodge, and with the hope that Esther Rogers was already at the over-look, armed with her own sketch pencils, furiously sketching the arch of a new day, she'd set out to find her.

Remind her that hiking out from camp without her counselor was a colossal no-no, even at Camp Blue Sky, and especially during the annual Ember Community Church family camp.

Even if the poor girl might be nursing a breakup.

Liza could murder heartbreaker Shep Billings with her bare hands. Or at least wound him with a graphite pencil.

Although, in her gut, Liza had a feeling Esther might have dreamed up Shep's attention toward her. The hot boys simply didn't date artsy, introverted, slightly chubby book nerds like Liza—*er*—Esther.

So, when Liza found the fifteen-year-old holed up last

night, face puffy, surrounded in wadded tissues, an early morning, brain-clearing hike up to the Snowshoe Mountain overlook to watch the sunrise over the hoary peaks seemed like something a savvy counselor might suggest.

Even as Liza hiked up to the overlook, the sunrise promised inspiration, clouds mottled with lavender and crimson, and gilded with the finest threads of gold feathered the heavens. A breeze tickled the aspen along the trail, the piney scent from the valley redolent with the heady sense of summer and freedom and fresh starts.

The air suggested another scorcher, dust and tinder-dry yellow needles kicked up on the path, settling onto her boots. Three weeks into her stay at Camp Blue Sky and already she'd seen two fires thicken the air above the Kootenai National Forest.

Most likely, the blond smokejumper was fighting some Glacier Park fire, sooty from head to toe, reeking of sweat and ash and wrung out from a week on the fire line.

At least that was how Conner most often came to her, in her dreams.

And there she went again, conjuring him up, as if he might swagger into her life, carrying a donut, a cup of coffee, and that languid smile that made her heart lie to her.

Enough.

The overlook hung over a ledge in the Pine Ridge trail, ten feet of cut-away granite edged with a cowboy split-rail fence for a modicum of protection from the two-hundred-foot drop. Further up, the trail banked around the edge of mountain, the land falling more gently into a valley until it tumbled into the north fork of the Bull River.

A roughhewn bench, smoothed out by early morning enthusiasts, perched in the middle of the overlook.

Liza had dearly hoped to spot Esther, with her mousy brown hair held back with a blue bandanna, dressed in her freshly tie-dyed shirt and grubby jeans, seated and drawing the dawnscape.

Empty. "Esther?"

Liza's voice had echoed in the blue-gold of the morning, scattering the shadows that bled through the trees.

Nothing but the shift of the wind in the trees, the scolding of a wood thrush.

Huh.

So maybe Esther hadn't broken the rules. Which meant she was still back at camp, maybe having gotten up early to use the showers. Except Liza had stopped there, too, on her way and nothing but a few spiders rustled around the long building in the silvery predawn hours. All seventy-five family campers still tucked soundly in their beds.

Except, of course, Esther.

Liza had stood there, finishing off her coffee, debating.

Now that she was here, she could settle down, take out her board and start a fresh sketch. Or—probably she should head back to camp, just to make sure Esther wasn't really holed up in the chapel, still weeping. Or maybe in the mess hall, loading up on Captain Crunch.

Yeah, she knew teenage girls. Especially the ones who wore their hearts pinned to their sleeves, bait for the first wily teenage boy to take a whack at it.

But that's why they'd hired her—not only to teach art, but because she knew the kind of trouble teenagers could conjure up, both real and imagined. And she might not have all the answers, but she had a desire to keep life from feeling so big they gave into the urge to run.

Maybe someday, too, she could teach herself that same

trick.

Liza had walked to the edge of the cliff, breathed in the ethereal impulse to open her arms, take flight. To soar, caught on the currents rising from the valley. To escape the weight of the aloneness that sometimes took her breath away.

I love the sunrise. It's Lamentations 3:22, over and over—

Conner, lurking in her brain again.

Wow, she missed him. A burning hole in her chest that she probably deserved.

Conner Young simply hadn't been into her.

Which made her exactly the right candidate to counsel poor Esther.

Liza had turned to leave when her gaze caught on something—neon blue.

In that second, Liza's heart turned to stone.

A Blue Sky camp jacket. Caught in a gnarled cedar clinging to the rocky edge, as if—blown? Snagged on a fall?

Her breath hiccupped, turned to ash as she peered over the edge—*please, God, no.* Pebbles and the slick loam of old needles and runoff littered the ground of the overlook—easy to slip on should someone lose their footing.

But she saw nothing below—no broken branches from the black spruce further below, no tumble of boulders evidencing an avalanche.

No broken body of a fifteen-year-old girl crumpled at the base of the cliff.

Liza couldn't help it. She leaned over the edge. "Esther!" Her voice rippled in the air, too much panic in it to deny.

She closed her eyes, listened.

Maybe the jacket didn't belong to Esther. Maybe days ago a camper had shucked it off, left it here. The greedy wind scooped it up, flung it over the cliff, maybe—

It was then that the huffing sound behind her made her stiffen. The wind raked up a smell behind her, earthy, rank, the scent of beast.

Liza held her breath, turned.

Oh—no—

Standing at the head of the trail, forty feet away, his dark eyes rimmed by a ruff of matted brown fur, powerful forearms pawing groves into the dirt, head swinging—

Grizzly.

Her brain formed around the word even as she moved back against the rail. Glanced down.

Suddenly, the jacket made terrible, gut-wrenching sense.

The bear reared up, pawing at the air.

And sorry, she hadn't a prayer of playing dead with the scream roiling up inside her.

Oh, God, please make me fast.

And, if she lived, maybe He'd give her the courage to rewind time, past the last thirty minutes, or last night, all the way to last year, to the moment when she'd run away from Conner Young.

And, this time, she'd stay.

And don't miss Susie May's newest series, Montana Rescue!

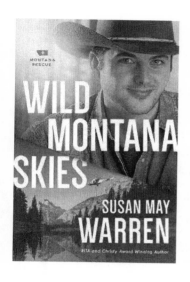
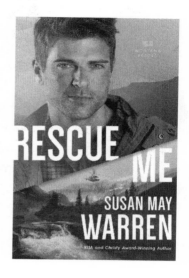

Visit www.susanmaywarren.com to get your sneak peek today!

Made in the USA
Coppell, TX
09 February 2020

15654819R00143